Invisible Death

Zarkon,

LORD OF THE UNKNOWN
IN

Invisible
Death

A CASE FROM THE FILES OF OMEGA,

AS TOLD TO

LIN CARTER

DOUBLEDAY & COMPANY, INC.
GARDEN CITY, N.Y.
1975

All of the characters in this book
are fictitious, and any resemblance
to actual persons, living or dead,
is purely coincidental.

Library of Congress Cataloging in Publication Data

Carter, Lin.
Invisible death.

I. Title.
PZ4.C3239Zaq [PS3553.A7823]   813'.5'4
ISBN 0-385-08768-3
Library of Congress Catalog Card Number 75-9219

Contents

Note

This is the second case from the files of the Omega organization which I have novelized in strictly documentary fashion. As was the case with the first, a book called *The Nemesis of Evil*, I have striven to reconstruct the precise sequence of events, working from extensive tape-recorded interviews with many of the leading participants in the adventure, and from the case records of Omega, for access to which I am deeply grateful to Prince Zarkon and to his lieutenants.

I should like to emphasize here that in all instances I have felt free to exercise the creative prerogatives of the novelist in my description of scene and character, and that many of the exchanges of conversation (indeed, virtually all) have been very freely reconstructed.

Because the investigations of the Omega group very seldom break into the headlines, and because the existence of the group is secret, most of my readers, if not all, will dismiss this book as purely a work of fiction. This does not in the least bother me. Nor will it affect the Lord of the Unknown and his associates, who have always tried to stay out of the spotlight, believing they can better fight organized supercrime if their cases remain unpublicized.

As I did in *The Nemesis of Evil*, I have changed the names of all persons and places in this book in order to protect their privacy. It goes without saying that there is no major center of population on the Eastern seaboard called Knickerbocker City, no communities on Long Island named Holmwood or Beechview, no police inspector named Ricks, no Constable named Gibbs, no lawyer named Seaton, and so on.

Because this particular sequence of events reminds me, in its color and flavor, of the marvelous stories Walter Gibson used to write in my boyhood for *The Shadow* magazine, I have not only taken the liberty of dedicating this book to him but I have amused myself by appropriating names and places from some of his stories and used them herein in lieu of names of my own coinage. Thus, the reader who happens to be a Shadow buff may recognize the fashionable suburb of Holmwood, Long Island, Wang Foo's tea shop on the squalid borders of Chinatown, the Grandville Building, and the Metrolite Hotel as places mentioned in *The Living Shadow*, which was the first of all of Walter Gibson's Shadow novels, while the exclusive Cobalt Club first appeared in *The Shadow Laughs;* the Beechview Country Club, investment broker Rutledge Mann, and the Badger Building figured in another Shadow novel called *Grove of Doom.* Fans of *Dr. Death, Doc Savage,* and *The Spider* be warned: I have continued to amuse myself in similar fashion throughout the writing of this book.

—LIN CARTER

Invisible Death

CHAPTER 1

Just a Death at Twilight

The country estate of millionaire industrialist Jerred Streiger was located in the fashionable and exclusive suburb of Holmwood, Long Island. It was a large, rambling building of Georgian red brick with white trim, situated on heavily-wooded acreage, locked away from the world behind towering walls of granite fieldstone, massive gates of wrought iron, and uniformed guards.

But walls, gates, and guards cannot lock out death. For the Grim Reaper strikes even the most closely guarded, even the most securely protected.

Perhaps that is why Jerred Streiger was so afraid. For he was indeed afraid: it showed in his wary, red-rimmed eyes, always darting nervously about from side to side; it showed in the way he started at shadows or jumped at unexpected noises. And it was there in his shaking hands, his sleepless nights, and the heavy Colt .45 he kept beneath his pillow.

Everyone at his country manor, Twelve Oaks, knew he was afraid of something—from Sherrinford the butler and Canning, his private secretary, to Chandra Lal, his Indian valet, and Borg, his bodyguard. But none of them knew the name of the thing he was afraid of . . . save that it came in little gray envelopes, the size you send party invitations in.

The little gray envelopes had started coming about two weeks ago. At first they had come two or three days apart;

now it had been several days since the last of them arrived. But when Sherrinford took the morning's mail from Pipkin the gatekeeper, there was a little gray envelope tucked among the letters. Like all the others, it bore neither stamp nor postmark.

Like all the others, there was no return address.

Sherrinford weighed it thoughtfully. He was strongly tempted to slit open the little gray envelope and look inside it. But he refrained virtuously from so doing; butlers did not read their masters' mail. Such things, quite simply, were not done.

So Sherrinford took the stack of letters, including the little gray envelope, upstairs to the master bedroom on the second floor, with the breakfast tray. He knocked quietly on the oaken panel, then opened the door and entered. Jerred Streiger was sitting up in bed, his strong-jawed, heavy face pale and haggard, his dark hard eyes red-rimmed from lack of sleep.

"The mail? Give it to me, man!"

Sherrinford placed the breakfast tray across his master's lap and stepped across the room to open the thick drapes.

The sound of a shattering crash from behind him jerked the butler around. His impenetrable mask of urbanity was broken by what he saw. Jerred Streiger had flung the tray to the floor. Orange juice soaked into the wet carpet; scrambled eggs and bits of sausage made a ghastly mess by the bedside.

Ghastlier still was the face of Jerred Streiger.

It was white as milk, that face. Sherrinford had fought in the trenches in the First World War; once before he had seen a man's face that unnatural color, but the man had been caught in No Man's Land, hung on the barbed wire. All night he had bled to death slowly, slowly; by dawn when they found him, his face was that same grisly pallor.

"Sir? Sir! Are you unwell? Shall I fetch Dr. Grimshaw?" gasped the butler.

But Jerred Streiger heard him not. Lips pale as paper, and as thin, moved feebly, whispering. The millionaire seemed to be repeating the same words over and over, in tones so weak the butler could barely hear them.

Sherrinford hurried to the side of the bed. The first thought that passed through his mind was that Jerred Streiger had suffered a stroke, a heart attack. But no, the millionaire waved him away irritably.

"I'm all right, you fool. Get out! Tell Borg I want to see him at once."

"Certainly, sir," said Sherrinford, his shocked features resuming their usual expression of serene imperturbability. Leaving the room, he turned to the intercom over a small side table in the hall, picked up the house phone, and dialed Borg's extension. A moment later the surly voice of the body-guard growled a query.

"Yeah? Whozis?"

"Sherrinford, Mr. Borg. The master wishes to see you in his private quarters at once," said the butler.

"He does, does he? Another of them little gray letters, hanh?"

"I'm afraid so," admitted Sherrinford. The voice on the other end of the line growled an oath.

"Cripes, I wish the boss'd call the cops—or do somethin'. Whaddaya think it is, blackmail?"

The butler's lips thinned in reproof. "I'm sure I do not know, Mr. Borg. I must go now. The master is expecting you . . ."

"Yeah, yeah! Jeez, lemme get some clo'es on, willya?"

Sherrinford hung up the phone and went downstairs. All the way down the stairs the whispered words he had heard hoarsely breathed over and over from the white lips of Jerred Streiger went tumbling through his mind. Their ominous import did not escape him. But for the life of him, Sherrinford could not guess their meaning.

You may expect the Grim Reaper at twilight.
You may expect the Grim Reaper at twilight.
You may expect the Grim Reaper at twilight.

After a leisurely breakfast, the wealthy inhabitants of Holmwood generally went about their business in an amiable,
unhurried fashion. For some, this meant a drive to the golf
course, the country club, the tennis court, or the marina on
Long Island Sound for a day of boating. Others, with more
pressing duties, went into the city to attend to such important things as board meetings or visits to the Stock Exchange
or the bank. Generally, these business matters were
concluded early enough for a long, leisurely luncheon at the
club, and then the drive home for preprandial cocktails.

But no one entered or left the locked and guarded gates of
Twelve Oaks for any reason. Like a fortress under siege, the
red brick mansion squatted amidst its grounds, surrounded
by high walls and iron bars and armed guards. No one came
in and no one went out—not even Mrs. Callahan, the housekeeper, who almost invariably went into town on Tuesdays,
driven there and back by Cramden the chauffeur for the
weekly shopping. And although she protested loudly and at
length, old Pipkin the gatekeeper remained adamant.

"No one comes in an' no one goes out—includin' yerself,
Missus Callahan," said the silver-haired old man staunchly.
"Them's me orders, and that's how it'll be, so help me! If
ye've any complaints, take them t' Mr. Canning, for he's th'
one as give 'em to me."

"Mr. Canning, is it?" fumed the housekeeper, her fat-
cheeked red face glaring belligerently. "Sure an' I'd loike to
know how a body's s'posed t' keep meat on th' table, if she's
not to go inta town t' buy it?"

But as the good woman soon found, no appeal to logic,
reason, emotion, or sentiment could sway the stouthearted
Pipkin one inch from strict obedience to his orders. Vocifer-
ously demanding the hosts of Heaven bear witness to the

way a body was put upon, Mrs. Callahan returned to the mansion house. But she did not pursue the matter with Canning, despite her threats to do so. She and the smooth-faced, bespectacled young male secretary did not see eye to eye on very many matters, and she refused to give the young man an opportunity to "lord it over a body," as she would put it.

The long, lazy summer afternoon wore on. Sunset flamed in the west, spectacularly lighting up the forested hills of the great estate. It came to the hour of dinner. Jerred Streiger was a heavy eater, but this evening he only picked distractedly at each dish before growling at Sherrinford to take it away. During the entire meal the long French doors which let out on the sunken garden remained closed and locked, despite the humid temperature, and Streiger had commanded his butler to draw the drapes.

Even stranger than this was the presence of Borg in the dining room. Such a thing had never happened before. The beefy, blue-chinned man in the ill-fitting suit had taken a seat behind Jerred Streiger and between the millionaire and the windows. He kept one huge, hairy hand in his pocket, as if holding a gun to the ready. It made Sherrinford nervous; and it reminded him of the message in the little gray envelope and what it had said about *twilight*.

And twilight was almost here.

After dinner, it was the invariable habit of the millionaire industrialist to take brandy and cigars in the library. This night proved no exception, except that Borg was bidden to accompany him into that hushed sanctum of gilt-edged books, fine-tooled bindings, thick carpets, first editions, and old masters.

Nervously puffing on a fine Havana, Streiger gulped rare brandy, looking again and again at the clock. Suddenly he turned to Borg, seated again near the long French doors, and harshly bade him call Canning to see that the floodlights were switched on. The bodyguard blinked at this unlikely command. He knew that Jerred Streiger had installed flood-lights so that they illuminated the exterior of the house from all angles; but it was not yet even dark—

"Do as I say, you hulking idiot!" snarled the millionaire ferociously. Shrugging, Borg left his post. The house phone was in the hall just outside the door. Borg never reached it. The sudden gasp of an inhaled breath and the clunk of a heavy crystal goblet falling to the thickly carpeted floor halted him in his tracks. He whirled, snatching out his gun, and stared back into the room he had just left.

Jerred Streiger lay crumpled on the floor.

His face was gray as the little square envelopes had been, and his eyes were rolled back into his head so that only the bloodshot whites were visible.

Borg had seen plenty of corpses in his time. He knew he was looking at one now.

Somehow, through stone walls and iron gates and armed guards, Death, the Grim Reaper, had reached his long arm to lay his invisible hand on the life of Jerred Streiger.

CHAPTER 2

The Omega Man

To a certain square block of rundown brownstone residence buildings on the West Side overlooking the Henry Hudson River, there are delivered every day an immense quantity of newspapers. Not only all five of the daily newspapers published in the city, but leading newspapers from Washington, Chicago, Boston, Philadelphia, Los Angeles, and other major centers of population in this country, and important newspapers from more than a dozen foreign capitals as well, are lugged to the green door with the small brass plate by perspiring postmen and delivery boys.

The rest of the houses on the block receive no mail at all, not ever. Because no one lives behind those other doors. The entire brownstone block is actually one enormous building, although this fact is disguised by the façade of false building fronts. Geraniums bloom in window boxes; lace curtains or drawn shades obscure the rows of windows; chimneys and television antennas bristle on the roof tops. But despite these facts, the entire block is one gigantic building, and that building houses the headquarters of the little-known Omega organization, one of the world's smallest and least-publicized crime-fighting agencies.

Very few know that behind that innocent-looking row of false fronts is a wall of battleship steel, braced to resist anything up to a General Sherman tank, or that the lace-curtained windows are of four-inch-thick, optically polished plexiglass that can stand up to anything this side of a mortar shell. And even fewer know that only five men and their mysterious master dwell within this private citadel, from which they conduct an unending crusade against crime.

It was the task of a huge, oafish-looking man with rumpled sandy hair, a pale freckled face, watery stupid-looking blue eyes, and outsized hands and feet to scan quickly through the contents of each of the thirty or more newspapers delivered daily to the headquarters of Omega.

The name of this man was Theophilus "Doc" Jenkins. To the casual glance he looked like a big dumb lummox. But those who accounted him as such were very much in error. For behind that pale, slab-sided, befreckled face reposed one of the most remarkable intellects on the planet. Yes, Doc Jenkins was one of those rare, extraordinary men with eyes like a camera, ears like a tape recorder, and a brain like a giant computer. It was physically impossible for him ever to forget anything he had seen or read or heard. Every tiniest shred of memory stored in that astonishing brain was ready for instant recall. He had developed his miracle memory to the point where he could not only read but completely commit to memory the contents of a book in fifteen minutes. And years later, when needed, he could quote page after page from that book without a moment's hesitation. He could even tell you the page number of the matter he was quoting.

With such a brain, it did not take Doc Jenkins long to search through the miniature mountain of newspapers and mentally index their contents. He paused from time to time, however, to mark with a red crayon certain news articles he thought might be of interest to his mysterious master.

On this particular morning, the papers were full of the sudden death of Jerred Streiger. The red crayon came out several times during the course of Doc's perusal of these papers. There were several odd things about the death of the

millionaire that seemed puzzling. For one thing, the doctor
who had examined the body less than twenty minutes after
Streiger's demise could not find any cause of death.

When a man turns gray and falls down dead on the spot,
heart failure is the first thing people think of. But not in the
case of Jerred Streiger. The industrialist had been in the full
vigor of his prime and strong as a bull. And he had a heart
that should have been good for another twenty years of
life.

For another thing, rumors were rife that Streiger had virtually become a recluse in recent weeks, shutting himself away
behind the stone walls and iron gates of Twelve Oaks like
a man who fears his life is in danger. Never exactly the most
gregarious of men even in the best of times, Streiger's curious
reclusive behavior lifted eyebrows among those who had
known him. It just had not been like Jerred Streiger to be-
have in such a manner.

Finishing his task, Doc Jenkins sorted the stack of newspapers out on a long inlaid table and turned as a remarkably
short man with a cheerful pug-nosed face and bright blue
eyes came strolling into the room. The unmistakable stamp of
the Emerald Isle was written all over the diminutive, swag-
gering redhead. All he needed was a long gray beard,
buckled shoes and a fresh shamrock in his lapel, and you
would have instantly taken him for a pugnacious leprechaun,
strayed somehow from the misty glens and bogs of Ireland.

His name was Aloysius Murphy Muldoon, and he was
indeed of pure Hibernian descent. But men who permitted
his slight build and scanty inches to fool them frequently had
cause to regret their error while spending the next few weeks
in hospital beds. For under the sobriquet of "Scorchy" Muldoon, the peppery little Irishman had been a bantamweight
pugilist of world renown. His flying fists had laid out men
nearly twice his size, both in and out of the prize ring.

"Hi, Doc, is the chief come up yet this mornin'?" inquired
the little redheaded boxer cheerfully.

"Nope," said Doc Jenkins in his dull, heavy voice. "You're up early, Scorchy. Couldn't sleep?"

The small man shrugged irritably. "It's this ever-lovin' inaction is after gettin' me down, Doc. When, oh when, are we goin' to see a little action? Faith, I'm gettin' so rusty I don't know when wuz th' last time I mixed it up nice an' hot!"

Doc Jenkins chuckled. It was all of three weeks since their last adventure had thrust them into dire and deadly peril in the mysterious caverns of a hollow mountain, among weird red-robed cultists who worshiped a messiah of evil called "Lucifer." They had been alternately gassed, trapped, kidnaped, carried off in invisible helicopters, and nearly slain by the uncanny "Hand of Death"—and Doc, for one, had been happy to have a little comfortable leisure in which to rest up before their next adventure began: but here was Scorchy, chafing for the next adventure with the last one scarcely over!*

Doc was about to remark on this when the telephone rang. The big man took the call while Scorchy helped himself to breakfast from the covered dishes on the sideboard. He was busily munching ham and eggs when Doc joined him for a third cup of coffee.

"Who wuz that on the horn?" inquired the fiery-thatched bantamweight.

"Ricks of Homicide," mumbled Jenkins around a mouthful of hot coffee. "The chief took it on his extension." Scorchy's bright blue eyes gleamed even brighter.

"Homicide, is it? Faith, is't possible we're about to see a little action around here at last?"

"It's more than possible; I'd call it probable," said a voice behind them.

The two men turned to look at the man who had just come through the secret door behind the bookshelves, where a

---

* The adventure of the red-robed cultists to which the passage above refers has been made into a book called *The Nemesis of Evil*, recently published by Doubleday.

private elevator had carried him from his sanctum below the building.

Prince Zarkon, chief of the Omega men, was tall and long-legged, with a superbly developed body whose musculature was of such marvelous symmetry as to go unnoticed by the casual glance. He was attired from head to foot in gun-metal gray, from his suede shoes to his whipcord jacket and slacks and gray turtleneck pullover. Even the meticulously arranged fringe of locks which adorned his lofty brow were of the same shade of gray. The manner in which these locks were curled over his high forehead gave him a curiously antique look, like one of the ancient Roman portrait busts in the International Museum.

But nothing could be further from the facts. No antique Roman, Zarkon was a man from the very distant future, sent back in time to undo the grim and terrible future world in which he had been born as the last of a line of experimental supermen. That distant world was a dying one, its resources exhausted from millennia of war, its dwindling populace brutalized by centuries of subjugation to cruel overlords, its winds and waves poisoned to the point of sterility from ages of neglect and rampant pollution. It had been the sudden rise to power of ruthless supercriminals preying on the superstitions of the masses through scientific trickery that had brought the dying world to so grim a twilight. To destroy such masterminds of supercrime before they could bring all of civilization down in a succession of feudal dark ages was the task to which Zarkon, Lord of the Unknown, had dedicated his life.

The five men who fought with him knew the astonishing secret of his uncanny origin in the far future. They looked upon him as their leader with reverence and awe, but also with love. Each of them had come to the end of his tether; one by one he had rescued them from the living death of drugs or alcohol or crime or madness. Together they stood against that future world of horror and impending doom: together they would rewrite the future by changing the past.

Zarkon studied them, keen magnetic black eyes under towering brows in a golden face of heroic masculine beauty. A superman bred to this purpose over centuries, he was always ready to take up his unending battle against evil anew.

"That was Detective Inspector Ricks of Homicide on the phone," said Zarkon. "He wants me to look into the death of a wealthy man named Jerred Streiger. Do the morning papers have anything on it?"

"*Do* they! They're full of nothin' else," said Doc Jenkins cheerfully. "I got 'em already marked for you, chief." Zarkon crossed to the big inlaid table and looked through the newspapers, one by one.

"I see by the obituary in the *Times* that Streiger used to belong to the Cobalt Club," he said thoughtfully. "That's interesting. Doc, I need a car. Is anybody up yet? What about Ace?"

"Haven't heard a peep outa him yet," admitted Jenkins. "But from the early hour he and Menlo got back from the Club Galaxy last night—this morning, I mean!—I'm not surprised. But Nick was prowlin' around just a while ago. Guess he can drive you where you want to go—"

"Hey, chief, what about me?" demanded Scorchy, aggrievedly.

"Poo!" snorted Doc Jenkins, "the chief wants to get there in one piece, you pint-sized pugilist! I'll call Nick to drive you, chief."

"That third-rate vaudevillian?" grumbled Scorchy, but only by way of automatic reflex. It was a standing joke among the men of Omega that the bantamweight boxer was such a bad driver that he could hardly go thirty yards without bumping into something—or somebody.

Doc thumbed a switch on the P A system and his voice went booming out through the laboratories and workshops and research facilities of Omega, summoning Nick Naldini to the garage. A moment later the hoarse whiskey-voice of the former stage magician and escape artist came rasping over the same hookup:

"Righto, Doc! I'll be delighted to have a little action at last." Then he added, with a nasty chuckle, "Eat your heart out, Scorchy Muldoon!"

CHAPTER 3

Who Will Be Next?

Zarkon selected from among his private fleet of automobiles a long black Supra limousine. With Nick Naldini at the wheel, they drove across town to the elegant marble façade of a turn-of-the-century building designed by Stanford White, which stood on one of the quiet side streets off fashionable Fifth Avenue. A discreetly lettered bronze plaque announced that this was the exclusive Cobalt Club.

Leaving the car and nodding to the silver-haired doorman, Zarkon entered the building, crossed the foyer, and entered the high-ceilinged lounge where the members generally gathered for cocktails before luncheon. The room was huge, dark, quiet; parquet floors were covered with superb Oriental rugs, the walls bore mahogany bookshelves lined with fine-tooled leather bindings agleam with gold. Elderly waiters brought drinks on silver trays to members ensconced in old-fashioned leather armchairs.

Zarkon glanced about, searchingly. The membership of the Cobalt Club was by no means limited to old families, wealthy socialites, and millionaire clubmen. True, the oldest, wealthiest, and most socially prominent families of Knickerbocker City were represented, but so were the ranks of the law, medicine, the arts and sciences. Men of importance and distinction in all branches of endeavor were numbered among the membership of the Cobalt Club; Zarkon himself had been elected a member during his first year in the city.

Across the lounge five men whom he knew were seated in a circle, chatting over cocktails. They were trim, tanned and fit, keen-eyed athletic men in their prime, despite the touches of gray in their hair which suggested they were well past their first youth. Zarkon crossed to greet them.

"Hello there, Wayne, Reid. Wentworth, Brooks, good to see you again. Cranston, how are you? Mind if I join you?"

"Not at all, please do," murmured Cranston, waving to an empty chair. He was a tall, hawk-faced man with lazy, hooded eyes and dark smooth hair flecked with gray; his long lean legs, impeccably attired, stretched out before him. On the third finger of his left hand a rare girasol smouldered in a plain gold ring. He twisted the ring on his finger absently as he chatted with his friends.

Zarkon seated himself and let Cranston order him a dry martini.

"We were discussing old Streiger's death," remarked Wayne, a square-jawed man going gray at the temples. "Presume you read about it in the morning papers?"

"Yes, I have," Zarkon acknowledged, accepting his drink from the waiter and lifting the glass in salute. "I was wondering about it, in fact. The newspaper accounts were rather sketchy. Did any of you happen to know him? Wayne, don't you and your ward have a summer home out in that part of Long Island?"

"That's right," nodded the square-jawed millionaire. "Dick's been away at college for some years now, and we hardly use it any more. I used to run into Streiger now and again, mostly out in the Hamptons. But we moved in very different circles and I hardly knew him."

Zarkon nodded, sipping his martini. He knew that the wealthy clubman very largely confined his interests and activities to the nearby metropolis of Gotham City, so this came as no surprise.

"I believe Cranston knew him," added Wayne. The lazy,

hawk-faced man shrugged, moodily twisting the girasol on his long finger.

"We used to run into each other at the country club now and then," said Cranston absently. "He made a fourth for bridge, sometimes played a round of golf. Just a nodding acquaintance, though; as Wayne said, he kept pretty much to himself and moved in other circles."

"Which country club was this?" inquired the Prince.

"The Beechview Country Club, near Long Island Sound. I go out there for golf occasionally. The courses out my way are very inferior." Zarkon absorbed this thoughtfully: he knew Cranston's estate was out in the country, near the town of Merwyn, New Jersey.

"Queer, his dying like that," Cranston added. "Man was strong as a bull. Looked as though he would outlast us all. If I weren't flying to San Francisco tomorrow, I might just look into it."

Cranston had an amateur's interest in criminology, Zarkon knew, and sometimes lent his aid to the police commissioner as a sort of consultant. Zarkon asked if Cranston's friend the commissioner had any leads on the case that hadn't been mentioned in the news. The tall man shrugged indifferently.

"Afraid I don't know the commissioner as well as I should, although I was on quite good terms with Weston, his predecessor. Perhaps Reid has some inside stuff; his paper has been playing up the case."

Reid, the wealthy publisher of the *Daily Sentinel,* shook his head reluctantly. "I'm afraid not, Prince. But I have some of my best reporters working on the case, and they may turn up something soon. I have to leave the city myself for a few days, but I can have my secretary, Miss Case, call you if any promising leads turn up."

"I would appreciate that very much," Zarkon said. "I'm particularly interested in the cause of death. I understand the coroner ascribes it to a blood clot—"

Reid chuckled suddenly. "Yes, my Filipino houseboy,

Kato, has a theory on that which might amuse you. He puts it down to what he calls 'jungle devil magic': Seems, in the islands, when a man dies mysteriously and from no known cause, they put the blame on the Filipino equivalent of voodoo."

The men chuckled. Brooks, the dapper lawyer with the prematurely gray hair, laughed, twirling his slim black sword cane. "That would hardly be admissible in a court of law," he grinned. "But it's an interesting theory! My associates and I are leaving for Peru day after tomorrow, or we might look into the mystery ourselves." Brooks, the senior partner of the distinguished law firm of Van Dusen, Drew, Brooks & Rummel, had a hankering for adventure and divided his time about equally between forensic problems in the courtroom and exploits and explorations in the far corners of the globe.

Wentworth, seated next to that Harvard-trained vision of sartorial splendor, spoke up next. "Personally, I'd like to know if there's any truth to the rumor that Streiger had been receiving threatening notes."

"What kind of threatening notes?" inquired Zarkon.

Wentworth shrugged. "My servant, Ram Singh, knows a fellow-countryman in Streiger's employ, a chap named Chandra Lal. Chandra Lal says the rumor among Streiger's staff is that the old man had been getting anonymous notes warning that unless Streiger signed over his stock holdings to a third party, he would perish from the 'Invisible Death,' whatever that may mean."

"That's the first I'd heard of this," admitted Zarkon with interest. "Did Streiger have extensive holdings?"

"I believe he did, mostly in Worldwide Steel," murmured Cranston. "I happen to know that because we both have the same investment broker, Rutledge Mann. His offices are in the Badger Building, and I used to run into Streiger's attorney, Josiah Seaton, in Mann's offices."

"That sounds like a promising lead for you, Zarkon," suggested Britt Reid. The Ultimate Man nodded thoughtfully. Wentworth glanced at his watch, downed the rest of his drink at a gulp, and rose to his feet.

"Have to be going," he said offhandedly. "Leaving for Chicago tomorrow, myself . . . have an, ah, a social engagement first."

Cranston smiled sardonically. "To be sure, Richard! Oh, would you be kind enough to give my warmest regards to Miss Nita Van Sloan during your, ah, social engagement? And my sincerest sympathies, as usual."

This parting shot made Wentworth flush; then he grinned good-naturedly and left. His long-standing engagement to the attractive young woman in question, which had been going on for some years, was a standing joke among his friends.

Zarkon turned to the dapper lawyer with the slim black cane.

"Brooks, do you happen to know where Streiger's lawyer has his offices?"

"Certainly, my dear Prince! He maintains a suite of offices in the Grandville Building," said the impeccably attired lawyer.

Zarkon thanked him quietly, finished off his drink, made his farewells, and was about to leave when Cranston, still twirling his girasol ring moodily, spoke up in a somber voice.

"I've an intuition Streiger was only the first," the hawk-faced man said, staring broodingly into the lambent radiance of the fire opal.

"Perhaps," Zarkon agreed.

"And that makes me wonder . . ." murmured Cranston, broodingly.

"Wonder what?" asked Wayne.

"Oh, nothing; nothing really," said Cranston, stretching lazily like a great cat and rising to his feet. "I do believe it is time for luncheon, and I am famishing for a bit of Antoine's filet of sole . . ."

The others finished their drinks and rose to join him.

Zarkon alone would not be lunching at the Cobalt Club that day, for the mention of threatening letters and of Streiger's lawyer, Josiah Seaton, had given him a hot lead which he wished to pursue without undue delay.

He strolled with his friends into the foyer and shook hands with them there. Cranston lingered behind while the other men went into the dining room.

"You intend to pursue this matter seriously, then, Prince?" inquired the wealthy amateur criminologist.

"I believe so; in fact, the authorities have asked for my help. The Long Island suburb where Streiger lived is out of the jurisdiction of the city police, but the Holmwood force is poorly equipped for this sort of an investigation. I had a call this morning from Detective Inspector Ricks of the Homicide Bureau, asking if I'd be interested in taking a look out that way. Nothing much is going on right now, so I see no reason not to help them out."

"Good man, that Ricks," murmured Cranston. "He did brilliant work on those Mandarin murders some years back . . . a pity I have to make that trip to San Francisco! I'm more than half inclined to look into this thing myself. Still, business is business; and I'm leaving the matter in the very best of hands, if you and your team are going to handle the investigation."

"Nice of you to say so," smiled Zarkon. "I'd still like to know what it was you were wondering a minute ago."

"I was wondering who will be next," said Lamont Cranston somberly.

CHAPTER 4

The Grim Reaper!

Nick Naldini was stretched out lazily on the front seat of the limousine, smoking a king-sized cigarette in an even more king-sized holder, when Zarkon came over. The lanky stage magician straightened up with alacrity.

"Any luck, chief?" he queried Zarkon in his hoarse whiskey-voice. "Any leads, I mean?"

Zarkon climbed into the car. "I don't know, Nick. It's just possible. Let's go."

"Righto! But where?"

"The Grandville Building. It's on the corner of—"

"Sure, I know where it is. Hang on!"

The limousine tooled away from the curb, glided around the corner, and merged into the stream of heavy traffic that flowed along Fifth Avenue.

"I guess nobody at the Cobalt Club saw Streiger much these days, eh?" asked Nick, conversationally. "I mean, the *Times* obit said 'former member . . .'?"

Zarkon nodded. "I spoke to the porter, the steward, and the doorman, on my way out of there, and to the treasurer a bit earlier," he admitted. "Jerred Streiger hasn't been to the club in a good six years, and stayed pretty much to himself, according to one of the members, Wayne, who has a summer home out in Holmwood. And another fellow, Cranston, directed me to Streiger's country club. Maybe we should follow these leads up before going out to the Streiger estate."

"Okay," grinned the former illusionist. "Here we are, chief. Chief, I can't park in this block, so I'll just drive around and keep circling till I see you come out, okay?"

"That will be fine, Nick. I won't be long," said Zarkon. The limousine pulled up to the curb and the Man of Mysteries got out and entered the lobby.

The Grandville Building had once been one of Knicker-bocker City's newest and tallest skyscrapers. But that had been in the thirties; forty years had passed it by, and buildings taller and newer had long ago eclipsed its eminence.

By now, however, it had assumed something of the importance of a relic. With the Chrysler, the Graybar, and the Chanin buildings, it was one of the few surviving architectural masterpieces of the Art Deco style; lovingly preserved and thoroughly refurbished, it was now a prestige address. Just to have an office in the Grandville Building meant something to the tradition-minded old families of the social register.

Josiah Seaton's office, suite of offices really, occupied most of one of the upper floors. Zarkon entered into a blond reception room. Everything was of almost the same color, which created a striking effect. The sumptuous carpeting was dark gold, the window drapes of a metallic bronze, the furniture Swedish Modern done in blond oak.

The receptionist, quite in keeping with the general décor, was also Swedish—and blond. She accepted Zarkon's card with murmured thanks. Although her eyes widened slightly on recognizing his name, she was too well trained to gasp or ogle. She vanished into an inner office, leaving Zarkon to admire a fine Van Gogh—one of the famous "sunflowers" sequence. A moment later she emerged.

"Mr. Seaton will see you now, Your Highness."

Nodding his thanks, Zarkon entered, to find the inner office as richly old-fashioned as the reception room had been starkly modernistic. A wine-red Bokhara carpet was on the floor; the walls were oak-paneled from floor to ceiling; rows of legal tomes marched along mahogany bookshelves, gold titles glinting in the subdued lighting.

"Prince Zarkon? A pleasure, sir! How may I serve you?" boomed a hearty voice. Behind a massive inlaid desk, a portly man with a round, beaming face framed in crisp, snowy hair rose ponderously to grasp Zarkon's hand.

His face was merry and crimson, his small eyes cheerful, shrewd, and ice-blue. He wore a dark gray suit with a vest and a string tie. A gold watch-chain stretched across his rotund middle; among the several fobs which dangled therefrom was an Elks insignia. Such an outfit had scarcely been seen in the city in forty years: Josiah Seaton was very like the building in which he maintained his offices. Both had mellowed with time into a tradition of elegance and quality, without aging or ever becoming quaint.

"It concerns your late client, Jerred Streiger," said Zarkon quietly. The merry, red-faced man sobered; his cheerful smile died on his lips.

"Please, sir, have a seat. There are some excellent perfectos in that humidor beside you," said the lawyer. "Jerred Streiger . . . yes, it was a terrible thing. Always understood his heart was strong as a dollar—not that the dollar itself is any too strong these days, with the world monetary situation what it is! . . . but forgive me for admitting that I don't understand why you have concerned yourself with Jerred's affairs?"

"Do you know who I am?"

"The former Prince of the small Balkan state of Novenia," nodded Josiah Seaton amiably, returning to his place behind the heavy inlaid desk and folding his chubby hands together on the blotter before him. They were exquisitely manicured, those fat-fingered hands, Zarkon noticed; and the solitaire that flashed on one thumb was at least ten carats of diamond. "As I recall, Novenia controls the world's only known source of some rare heavy metal or other which is vital to the manufacture of nuclear weapons and to the production of atomic power. You restored the healthy economy of your country by introducing a cheap, fast, and easy method for refining the vital ore, then established a model democracy, wrote a constitution that is still a marvel to the students of political science, and abdicated to enter this country on a permanent visitor's passport with full diplomatic immunity. You reside on the West Side, own a small island in the Hudson River, where you maintain a miniature fleet of private planes and ships, and are reputed to have an immense private fortune that makes the Rockefellers look like parvenues by comparison."

Zarkon could not help being impressed. He grinned and ducked his head in tribute. "That's the best thirty-second dossier I've ever heard," he smiled. "I begin to understand, Mr. Seaton, why you have the reputation you do."

The lawyer chuckled good-humoredly. "In my profession, Your Highness, it pays to know a lot—about a lot of things! But come, sir. You wanted to see me in connection with Jerred Streiger. What is it that I can do for you?"

"I need information, and badly," said Zarkon. "There is reason to assume that Jerred Streiger's death was not, well, not a natural one."

"Murder, you mean?" The lawyer's voice was a mere whisper. He looked shocked. "I've heard nothing of this! The police made no such suggestion. I understood it was a stroke of some kind . . ."

"Apparently it was, but possibly one induced by some exterior means. I have yet to see the coroner's report, or talk to Streiger's doctor, who was the first to examine the body after his demise."

Josiah Seaton's eyes remained shocked, his voice shaken, but his round red face assumed an expression grimly truculent.

"If someone killed Jerred Streiger, sir, I will lend you every possible assistance, merely for the asking, to apprehend the villain. We were attorney and client, yes; but we were also the best of friends for nearly thirty-five years. Anything I can do to assist you in discovering the scoundrel—!"

"I will accept your offer of help with gratitude," said Zarkon. "First, I would be interested in learning exactly who will benefit the most from his death. If you were close personal friends with Streiger, then you must know his family quite well."

"Of course," nodded Josiah Seaton. "What's left of the family, that is. Jerred's wife, Eleanor, predeceased him by more than twenty years. And their only child, a son named Obadiah, was killed in the Second World War. A major in the Air Force, as I recall. Jerred has no living brothers or sisters. There *is* a nephew, but Jerred and he haven't been on speaking terms for ten years. The young man, Caleb Streiger by name, has not the slightest interest in stocks and bonds and securities; his one consuming passion is radio. He is something of an inventor in that line and maintains a small laboratory downtown on Graumann Street, I believe."

"Is the nephew Jerred Streiger's only heir? As Streiger's attorney, you must know the terms of his will. I suppose I'm asking you to betray a confidence, but if you don't mind bending the ethics of the bar just a bit, learning who will profit from his death might go a long way towards establishing just who had the strongest motive."

Josiah Seaton fingered his chin unhappily, then shrugged. "Ethics, be hanged! Murder is murder, in my book. But you can forget about Caleb Streiger, Your Highness: he inherits a modest income from stock in Worldwide Steel, but nowhere near enough to murder a man for—even if 'that tinkering idiot'—as poor Jerred used to refer to him, with an invariable snort of derision—had it in him to commit murder, which I can't believe. No—there are a great many minor bequests— old servants, old friends, various charities. But no one individual stands to inherit any truly substantial amount, I'm afraid."

"To whom does the bulk of the fortune go, then?" asked
Zarkon.

"Well, to the Streiger Foundation. The foundation will inherit almost everything except for the estate house and its
furnishings and the minor cash or stock bequests. The house
and the furnishings go to Caleb Streiger. Not that they aren't
worth a tidy sum, of course, what with the current value of
Long Island real estate these days."

After a few more questions, Zarkon inquired if Josiah Seaton
had heard the rumor about the so-called threatening letters
which Jerred Streiger had supposedly been receiving for the
two weeks prior to his death.

Josiah Seaton's reaction to the question was alarming, even
startling. He turned pale and his hands jerked suddenly in a
spasm which sent a heavy carved malachite ashtray thudding
to the carpet. Zarkon retrieved it, replacing it on the desk.
Breathing hoarsely through half-open lips, Josiah Seaton
stared beyond Zarkon into empty space. From the haunted
expression in his eyes, he obviously dreaded what he saw
there.

"That explains it, then," he breathed gaspingly.

"Explains what?"

"Explains why he said nothing of this matter to me. Why,
the first thing Jerred Streiger would have done, had anyone
been sending him threatening letters, would have been to
call me and tell me about them. But . . . of course! . . . he
remembered the murder of Pulitzer Haines!"

"Who was Pulitzer Haines?" asked Zarkon.

The attorney fixed him with a glance of surprise. "The
Iranian Oil millionaire . . . he died the better part of a month
ago . . . of a massive stroke, they said. But it was common
knowledge that his life had been threatened by some mad-
man calling himself 'the Grim Reaper.' And everyone knew
that the notes from the Grim Reaper were written on gray
paper in little square gray envelopes . . ."

Zarkon frowned; it was not like him to have missed hearing of such an odd occurrence. But a moment's reflection made him realize that about the time that Pulitzer Haines had been receiving letters from the mysterious killer, he and the Omega men had been thousands of miles away in California, hot on the trail of the mad scientist, Lucifer.

The Grim Reaper . . .

Something about that odd name sent a chill up Zarkon's back.

CHAPTER 5

Zarkon Investigates

Another of those interminable king-sized cigarettes was smouldering in the long metal cigarette holder clenched between Nick Naldini's teeth as Zarkon left the Grandville Building and entered the black limousine.

He directed the stage magician to drive him to the estate of Jerred Streiger in Holmwood, Long Island, and settled himself in the rear seat. A slight frown of thoughtfulness knit his brows; his magnetic black gaze was brooding. Then, reaching a decision, he opened a compartment in the back panel of the front seat and took out the receiver of a mobile telephone. He dialed the private unlisted number of Omega headquarters.

A moment later Doc Jenkins was on the line.

"Doc, this is the chief. I have just concluded a meeting with Josiah Seaton in the Grandville Building; he was Jerred Streiger's attorney. He informs me that Streiger's only surviving relative is a nephew, Caleb Streiger. The young man stands to inherit a small sum, but check him out anyway. The works, including the District Attorney's office and the Justice Department in Washington. Oh, you might ask Menlo if he knows anything about him. The boy is something of a radio bug, and an inventor in that field. Check the patent office when you're on the line to Washington and find out if he holds many patents on inventions, and what the inventions are."

"Right, chief!"

"Then call Herrimann at the Securities Exchange Commission and find out all you can about the Streiger Foundation—its worth and its holdings."

"Right again, chief."

"I'm going out to Streiger's estate now, and will be there the rest of the afternoon. I'll be talking to the doctor who examined the body—what was his name, again?"

"Grimshaw. Ernest Grimshaw, it says here."

"All right. You might send Scorchy and Ace out in the Vanzetti. Have them register at the local motel or whatever. They should check with me when they arrive, either at Streiger's phone number or on the mobile unit, as I may be in transit."

"Sure—Scorchy's right here, rarin' to go," chuckled Doc Jenkins. "Ace says to ask you what equipment you want him to bring."

"I really don't know what we'll be getting into," said Zarkon, "so tell him to bring all the standard gear. Oh yes; equipment case three might come in handy."

"Case three it is, chief. Good hunting!"

"One thing more," Zarkon added. "Check your newspaper files for accounts of the death of another millionaire named Pulitzer Haines, who died almost a month ago under very similar circumstances, according to Josiah Seaton. Make a digest of all pertinent data, then call Ricks at Homicide for the official police file on Haines' death. You can shoot it to me on the fax outlet here in the mobile unit, or have Ace and Scorchy bring it out when they come, whichever is quicker. Got that?"

"Got it. Pulitzer Haines! Jeez, boss, what a moniker! How could I have missed that one . . . guess we were out spookin' around Mount Shasta after Lucifer and his gang about that time, is how. Well—good hunting, once again!"

Zarkon hung up the phone and sat back to do some thinking.

He put through three more phone calls, one to the Constable's office in Holmwood to find out the location of the coroner's office and the town morgue where the body of Jerred Streiger supposedly was, and also for the street address of Dr. Grimshaw's office.

The body, he learned, was already in the hands of the local undertaker and preparations for the funeral were underway. That was regretful, for once the body had been embalmed he could not perform an autopsy to discover the precise cause of death. Well, he could only hope that Dr. Ernest Grimshaw had done a thorough autopsy on Streiger's corpse, and kept detailed records of his findings. The Constable's office gave him the address of the physician.

Then he sat back and thought long and hard.

Nick took the Midtown Tunnel and then the expressway, turning off at Herkwell. As they drove along, the greenery got progressively more cultivated, the houses larger and more elaborate, the streets more rustic and also more immaculate. It was obvious that these homes were in the hundred-thousand-dollar bracket, and the further out they went, the more expensive everything became. Finally, they were driving past walled country estates built on property so extensive that the houses were not even visible from the road.

They came to the fieldstone wall surrounding Streiger's estate, Twelve Oaks. They followed it to an elaborately worked gateway consisting of twin pillars surmounted by heraldic lions, with a scrollwork gate of wrought iron that must have been a dozen feet high. Naldini hopped out and rang the bell. An elderly man with clear tanned features, sharp blue eyes, and silvery hair emerged from the gatehouse to look them over. Under one arm, fully cocked, he carried a twelve-gauge shotgun, and a Webley pistol was holstered at his hip. Zarkon and Naldini displayed their credentials, which bore several

startlingly famous signatures, including those of the Gover-
nor and the President. They had no trouble in gaining entry.

They drove slowly up the winding gravel driveway to the
huge Colonial house. The drive took all of ten minutes, which
may suggest the extent of Streiger's private acreage. The
drive was lined with trees on either side, spaced about
twenty-five feet apart. Nick Naldini whistled in awe.

"Wonder why the old fellow called this joint Twelve
Oaks," he murmured. "Twelve *Hundred* Oaks would be
more like it! This guy owned enough land to build another
whole town as big as Herkwell, back there at the turnoff."

The butler, Sherrinford, opened the door as they were
coming up the steps; obviously Pipkin the gatekeeper had
called the house to announce they were on their way. Zarkon
said nothing, but he admired Streiger's thoroughness in the
matter of security measures; obviously, it would have been
considerably difficult for any outsider to get in unannounced
and undetected. The height of the walls surrounding
Streiger's property, the guard dogs he had seen roaming
about from the car, and carefully positioned floodlights
which illuminated the exterior of the house at night, all of
these suggested this would not have been the easiest house in
the world to burgle.

The police had left long ago, concluding their investigation
of the house and the grounds. But Sherrinford had been
apprised by them of Zarkon's impending arrival, and of his
authority to investigate the case. Inspector Ricks of
Homicide must have called the local Constable, an officer
named Oglethorpe Gibbs, as soon as Zarkon had replied
favorably to his request that the Omega men look into the
matter of Streiger's death.

Sherrinford escorted them to the study where the body
had been found, and summoned Borg to be interviewed. The
heavy-set bodyguard was surly and belligerent, but subdued.
Zarkon let Nick Naldini ask him the more obvious questions,
listening keenly all the while, as he prowled about the room

with Sherrinford hovering at his elbow. The position in
which Streiger's body had been found had been outlined by
the police with white chalk—to the considerable detriment of
a fine carpet. The body had lain about thirteen feet from the
French windows.

Zarkon went over to examine them.

"Were these drapes drawn at the time of Streiger's death?"

"Yes, sir," said the butler. "Exactly so; nothing in the room
has been changed. Everything is just as it was the evening
the master died."

Zarkon studied the fabric of the drapes, held them to his
nostrils, then drew them aside and examined the windows
themselves. He studied them under a powerful lens with the
aid of a small but intense flashlight beam; then he opened
them and stepped outside to look around the neatly clipped
shrubbery and examine the ground.

Re-entering the room, he asked as to the weather.

Sherrinford was too discreet to permit curiosity to show in
his imperturbable visage, but he repeated the question with a
rising tone indicative of a query.

"It has been clear and dry for some days, sir," said Sherrinford at last.

Zarkon nodded and turned to other matters.

"Sherrinford, I would like from you a complete list of
every person on the estate—everyone who was here the night
your master died, down to the least important servant. Can
you do that for me?"

"Certainly, Your Highness; it will be a pleasure."

The butler departed to draw up the list; Zarkon turned to
Naldini, who had just let the bodyguard leave.

"Nothing much from him, I gather?" he murmured.

Nick shrugged. "Seems like a straight guy, but you never
know. Want me to check him out with the authorities?"

"Later. After I've had a look at the complete list of the staff
which the butler is making for me now; we may have several
names to check on."

A pert-faced maid ducked around the door. "Excuse me, sir! Telephone for you; you c'n take it in the foyer, if you wish." Zarkon did so. It was Scorchy Muldoon; obviously, he and Ace Harrigan had wasted no time in driving out, themselves.

Zarkon told them to unpack and circulate: talk to bartenders and old men sunning themselves on park benches, and other good sources of information. "I'd like to know if any strangers were in the vicinity a day or two before Streiger's murder," he said.

The silence at the other end of the line was deafening. Then—

"So ye do be after thinkin' it *wuz* murder, chief?" asked Scorchy excitedly. Whenever the feisty little Irishman became excited, he "got his Irish up," as he himself would put it. This generally took the form of a bit of the old Irish brogue, which tended to creep into his voice on such occasions.

"I know it was," said Zarkon evenly. "In fact, I know how it was done—I think."

CHAPTER 6

Another Victim

It was mid-afternoon by now. As neither Zarkon nor Nick
Naldini had been able to afford the time for luncheon, they
accepted Sherrinford's offer and let him serve them an early
dinner. As they ate, Zarkon read over the list of the staff of
Twelve Oaks which he had asked the butler to prepare for
him; he had made a special request that Sherrinford note
which of the staff members were recent additions, and how
recent.

This information looked to be rather disappointing, at first
glance anyway. Only two servants had been added to the
staff within the last six months, and neither of them seemed
to amount to much. One was a Chinese boy, hired to help the
gardener, the other an upstairs maid named Brigid O'Toole.

After their meal, Zarkon briefly questioned each member
of the Twelve Oaks staff in the study, spending only a couple
of minutes on each. Nick Naldini watched, smiling to himself: he admired the smooth way Prince Zarkon set each servant at his or her ease. A simple handshake did it, a smile,
and a friendly clap on the shoulder. In no time such tactics
had them telling him their life histories. From none of them,
however, did Zarkon learn much of anything that was of
bearing on the case, as far as Nick could tell.

Canning, Streiger's secretary, was a cold, personable
young man with a pronounced Harvard accent and a manner
in which, oddly, both obsequiousness and superciliousness

were blended. Mrs. Callahan, the housekeeper, Cramden the chauffeur, Halloway the chef, these people contributed little or nothing of value. Streiger, they said, kept to himself, never entertained, had few friends. He had been a frightened man in fear of his life since the first of the little gray envelopes had appeared with the morning mail. None of them had ever seen the Grim Reaper's notes, but all were aware of them.

Borg, the surly bodyguard, and Sherrinford the butler, Zarkon had already interviewed; but Chandra Lal, Streiger's devoted valet, proved useful. The Hindu was tall and swarthy and bearded, his head wrapped in a turban of yellow silk. Zarkon addressed him in Hindustani, and his eyes lit up at being spoken to by a sahib in his native tongue.

"To be certain, sahib, this person has seen the little gray letters," the Hindu said in reply to Zarkon's question. "Very often one would still be about my master's quarters when this person came to array him for the day. But never for long; always he burned such in the place-of-fire." By this he meant the black marble fireplace in Streiger's suite, most likely.

Zarkon looked the tall Rajput over thoughtfully, liking what he saw. The Rajput were a warrior race; the blood of ancient kings ran in their veins. Seldom was a Rajput willing to accept such menial labor as becoming a bodyservant; but when one did so, it was for life. Their race worshiped the principle of loyalty as other races worship gold or pride or power.

"You are a friend to Ram Singh, who works for my friend Wentworth, are you not?" inquired the Man of Mysteries, still speaking flawless Hindustani.

The tall Rajput grinned, white teeth flashing.

"Is it possible that the sahib knows Ram Singh, my friend and fellow-countryman?" he asked. Zarkon shook his head.

"I have not had that pleasure, Chandra Lal," he said quietly. "But I know that Ram Singh is loyal to my friend Wentworth, and I know that my friend would unhesitatingly trust your fellow-countryman with his life, if need be. Is it possible that I can trust you to the same extent?"

Chandra Lal drew himself erect. His eyes were proud, like a hawk's. "My master was a hard man, but fair and just; I loved him. And he respected Chandra Lal and gave him his trust. Now he is dead and you seek the lowly pig who struck him down. For that reason, you may ask anything of Chandra Lal—even his life!"

Zarkon nodded. "I thought as much. Listen to me, Chandra Lal: someone who lives here at Twelve Oaks murdered your master. I want you to be my eyes and my ears—watch, look, listen! Will you do that for me?"

"Sahib, I will do the thing you ask," said the tall Hindu simply. Zarkon smiled, clapped him on the shoulder; the Hindu saluted and left. Nick, who knew nothing of the language in which they had been speaking, asked, "Now, what was all *that* about?"

"I think we now have an ally in the servants' hall," Zarkon said. "A man whom we can trust . . . would you send in the next one, Nick?"

Nick ushered in the next servant and then went to check the car to see if the data Zarkon had requested was coming over the facsimile setup yet. Finally it did come rolling out of the slot; he brought it to Zarkon, who was chatting with the young Chinese undergardener at the moment. Seeing the fax print-off in Nick's hand, Zarkon dismissed the youth with a friendly smile and a clap on the shoulder. The youth displayed white molars in a delighted, if toothy, grin and sidled from the room. The Lord of the Unknown studied the police report briefly.

"A bad business, Nick," he said grimly. "But about the same as with Streiger. Threatening letters in little gray envelopes warning Pulitzer Haines to sign over his controlling interest in Trans-Iranian Oil to a third party, or be visited by the Grim Reaper. He was terrified, but blabbed about the threatening letters to the authorities. The Grim

Reaper came for him, just as he came for Jerred Streiger. Died of a stroke; no known history of heart trouble, and the coroner's report shows his arteries were in fine shape and his heart a remarkably healthy one for a man of his age. Get the car."

"Yowsah, boss! Where to?"

"Dr. Grimshaw's office. It's a bit late to find him in, but doctors don't keep bankers' hours. Oh, on your way out, ask Sherrinford for the name and address of the employment bureau or bureaus he uses to fill positions on the staff, will you?"

"Will do," said the lanky magician.

One of Streiger's servants brought the long black limousine around to the carriage drive where Prince Zarkon and Nick Naldini were waiting. Just as they were getting into the car, Sherrinford joined them on the steps.

"Will you be back this evening, sir?" the butler inquired. "I mean, will you be spending the night here? I have taken the liberty of asking the housekeeper to prepare rooms in the east wing for you and your associate."

"That was thoughtful of you, Sherrinford. Actually, I cannot say for certain, but it is more than likely that we shall be back by nightfall."

"Very good, sir." The butler started to turn away but Zarkon called him back.

"Oh, Sherrinford, there is one more thing I would like you to do for me."

"Yes, sir?"

"Is it possible for anyone here at Twelve Oaks to leave the grounds without your knowledge?"

The butler considered the question. "Yes, sir, it is *possible*. But rather unlikely. I am by way of being in charge of the staff, as I'm sure Your Highness will understand; it is I who apportion the work and see that it is done. At any given moment, I know where each member of the staff is and what he or she is then engaged in doing. Certain members of the staff do leave the grounds from time to time, with my knowledge and permission, either to have their day off, according to a fixed schedule, or to perform an errand. However, of course, one or more of the staff members *could* leave the grounds clandestinely, which is to say, without my knowledge or permission."

Zarkon absorbed this thoughtfully.

"But the gatekeeper would be aware of their leaving, wouldn't he?"

"He would, sir. There is no way to leave the property, other than by the gate. And, as the gate is kept locked at all times, Mr. Pipkin would have to let them in or out."

"I see . . . In that case, Sherrinford, I would be obliged if you would call Pipkin just as soon as I leave, and ask him to inform you the moment *any member* of the staff leaves the grounds for *any* purpose. Will you do that for me?"

"Of course, sir."

"Very good." Zarkon took out one of his cards and wrote two numbers on the back, handing the small pasteboard rectangle to the butler.

"The first number is that of the mobile telephone unit installed in my car. Call me at that number first, should anyone leave. The second number you will perhaps recognize as that of the inn in town; if you are unable to pass the information to me, call the second number and ask to speak to either of my associates, Mr. Muldoon or Mr. Harrigan."

"I will follow Your Highness' instructions to the letter."

"Thank you, Sherrinford!"

They pulled away from the steps. Gravel crunched under the wheels as the big limousine traversed the length of the drive. The silver-haired gatekeeper opened the gates for them and touched his brow respectfully as they drove out.

"You think it was an inside job, then, eh chief?" inquired Nick Naldini.

"It seems very likely. Streiger's security arrangements are

quite thorough and professional. It would have been pretty difficult for an outsider to gain entry unobserved."

Zarkon took out the mobile phone and called his headquarters in Knickerbocker City. A dry, irritable voice, which he recognized as that of Mendell Lowell "Menlo" Parker answered.

"Menlo, I'm going to need you and Doc out here after all. Take the big copter. In my private laboratory on the first sublevel you will discover the new long-range location-finder I have been working on. It will be set up on the lab bench near the generator. You should be able to dismantle it without trouble, I am sure."

"Okay," said Menlo, sounding somewhat more amiable than usual at the prospect of seeing a little action.

"We will also need the big city grid which includes all five boroughs. I don't know how you're going to get that into the copter—"

"Oh, we'll manage, chief," said Menlo. "Chief, you tested the new setup yet?"

"Not yet, unfortunately," Zarkon admitted. "But I have a feeling that we're going to be giving it a workout very soon. When you land at the Streiger estate, ask the butler, Sherrinford, for a large room in which to set up the new location-finder. A studio room with a skylight, or one of the stables or other outbuildings might be best. Keep in touch with me on the mobile unit; if I'm unavailable, call Scorchy or Ace at this number."

Again he repeated the number of the Holmwood Inn. Then he signed off.

The big limousine purred quietly through winding, tree-lined lanes. They had nearly reached town when an incoming call aroused the Omega Man from his thoughts. It was Menlo Parker.

"Just about to leave, chief, when we got a call from the office of the publisher of the *Daily Sentinel*," said the acerbic little scientist. "Seems urgent. Shall I patch it through the net to your unit?"

"Go ahead," said Zarkon. A moment later he heard the pleasant contralto voice of a young woman.

"Prince Zarkon? This is Miss Case speaking; Mr. Reid's secretary?"

"Yes, Miss Case?"

"Mr. Reid had to leave this afternoon on private business, but before he did so he asked me to keep you apprised of any new developments in the Streiger case."

"That was very thoughtful of him," said Zarkon warmly. "I assume from your call that there is something new on the case?"

"I believe so, sir. One of our reporters investigating the matter has called in with word that a second wealthy industrialist has just received a threatening letter on gray stationery from someone who signs himself 'the Grim Reaper.'"

Zarkon's magnetic eyes blazed with black fires. But when he spoke his voice was controlled. "His name?"

"Ogilvie Mather. He owns the Magnum Publishing Syndicate."

"I see. His address?"

"We are uncertain just where he is at this time," the girl confessed. "Mr. Mather has an estate in Beechview, Long Island, overlooking the Sound. He also maintains a suite in the Metrolite Hotel in the city, and has a summer place upstate on Lake Carlopa. We're checking right now to find him."

"Thank you very much for this information, Miss Case! I would appreciate hearing from you just as soon as you locate him." He gave Britt Reid's secretary the phone number of the mobile unit.

"Just a moment, sir," the girl said suddenly, just as Zarkon was about to hang up. When her voice came on again, it was vivid with excitement.

"One of our reporters on the case, Ned Lowry, just called

in. Ogilvie Mather is spending the weekend at his Beechview estate!"

"That's not far from here, chief; we can be there in a half hour or so," muttered Nick Naldini from the front seat, where he was listening in on the headset.

"Thank you, Miss Case," said Zarkon. "Let me return Mr. Reid's favor by passing along an item of information which I have recently learned. Jerred Streiger was not the first to be threatened and then murdered by the Grim Reaper; have your man Lowry look into the death of Pulitzer Haines about three weeks ago. He received the same kind of threatening letters, and he also died of a stroke or heart attack, without having any prior history of coronary trouble."

The girl thanked him and hung up.

"What d'you say, chief, shall we look into this Mather thing?" inquired Nick Naldini, eager for a little excitement.

"I think we should," said Zarkon keenly. "We can always interview Dr. Grimshaw later; it's really just a routine follow-up."

"If it's _that_ routine," grinned Nick, showing his long horsy teeth, "let Muldoon handle it. The pint-sized pugilist can't possibly bollix up anything that simple!"

Zarkon repressed a smile. Actually the warmest and closest of friends, the Mephistophelean vaudeville magician and the feisty Irish bantamweight had been conducting an open-end verbal duel for years. "I think I will do just that, Nick," he said, reaching for the phone again.

The long black limousine turned into a private driveway, backed out, turned around, and headed down the road toward Long Island Sound and the exclusive Beechview community.

CHAPTER 7

The First Warning

Sunset blazed gloriously in the west as the long black Supra pulled up before the Mather estate. A police car was parked in the drive, the red light atop its roof revolving. Nick and Zarkon were greeted at the door by a beefy, broad-shouldered young man with china-blue eyes and straw-yellow hair. His neatly pressed chinos, Sam Browne belt, holstered revolver, and badge denoted him as Oglethorpe Gibbs's deputy.

"Yassuh," said the youth with a pronounced Dixieland drawl, giving Zarkon a snappy salute. "Constable's inside a-talkin' t'Mister Mather. Y'all come along in."

"Is this Long Island or Manure Pit, Georgia?" asked Nick Naldini in a hoarse whisper which terminated in a chuckle. "I haven't heard an accent like that one since the Swamp Monster affair in Okefenokee!"

They entered a paneled hall. Crystal chandeliers shed a brilliance upon gilt-framed oils of the Hudson River School and the fine bindings of an excellent collection of first editions. Before a Florentine fireplace of carven marble, the Constable was deep in conversation with a nervous, rabbity little man in an expensive Bond Street suit. His garb was impeccable, but he himself was considerably less than pre-possessing. Pallid scalp showed through carefully arranged wisps of dingy hair; melting brown eyes that looked as if they belonged to a spaniel blinked continuously. He clasped and unclasped clammy-looking hands, and his mouth, thin, lip- less, and colorless, worked with a nervous tic.

"—My nerves can't stand it, I tell you! I'm not going to die as poor Streiger did—no, not me—I'll give him whatever he wants, I will— oh, dear, *what* is it *now?*" the rabbity little man squeaked as he spied Zarkon and Naldini enter.

"Oggie, this-here's Prince Zarkon an' his 'sociate," drawled the tall blond deputy.

The Constable turned to greet the Ultimate Man. Where his Georgia-spawned deputy had been immaculate, the county Constable was slovenly. His chinos were wrinkled and had grass stains on their sagging knees; his paunch bulged over his scratched black leather gun belt and strained at the shirt-buttons. He had a two days' growth of beard, a long knobby face, and wore a sweat-soaked and disreputable stetson hat. Even his badge, Nick noted, was unshined and dingy-looking.

"I know who hit is, Redneck, blast it!" the sloppy man said grumblingly. He touched two fingers to the sagging brim of the stetson, which he wore pushed well back on his head, exposing a grimy, gleaming, knobby brow. "Prince, you seemta hear about things quicker'n I do . . . this-here's Mr. Mather; Mr. Mather, this-here's Prince Zarkon of th' Omega agency, helpin' us out with this mess on behalf of th' city Homicide Bureau . . . show'm th' letter, Redneck, blast it all! This-here's my nevvy from Gawrgya, Prince; name of Red- ford Pickett. Family calls'm Redneck."

Zarkon greeted Ogilvie Mather quietly. The jumpy little man in the impeccable suit gave him a damp, listless hand- shake. The Georgia-born deputy, grinning embarrassedly, dug a small gray envelope out of his rear pocket and handed it to the Nemesis of Evil. Leaving Nick Naldini to elicit per- tinent data from Ogilvie Mather and Constable Oglethorpe Gibbs, the Prince crossed over to a petite French Empire desk, switched on a desk lamp, and subjected the contents of the square little envelope to a careful scrutiny under his powerful lens. The gray notepaper bore a Hammerville Bond watermark, which meant that it could have been purchased virtually anywhere, in any of thousands of department stores or stationery shops across the country. The message, neatly lettered with a heavy black felt-tipped pen, read as follows:

> *Pulitzer Haines and Jerred Streiger ignored my warnings. They suffered the Invisible Death, and are no more. You are next, Ogilvie Mather! Sign over your holdings in the Magnum Publishing Syndicate to the Pan-Global Corporation, Geneva, Switzerland; and deliver the stocks themselves and the transferral certificate to the red brick house on the corner of Mountainair and Farmwell Streets in uptown Knickerbocker City. The house is vacant. Just insert the papers through the mail slot in the front door. Do this and you will live, Ogilvie Mather. Fail to do this, and you will meet the Invisible Death. This is the first of seven warnings from—*
> *The Grim Reaper*

After a few reassuring words to the rabbity Mather, Zarkon left the house. Constable Oglethorpe Gibbs and his nephew Redneck joined the two Omega men at their vehicle. The dilapidated officer looked vaguely embarrassed; he tugged at the end of his long nose and scuffled his shoes in the gravel-strewn driveway.

"Sure am glad to have yer help on this baby, Prince," he said. "Really outa moh league this time. Never git nothin' much out here, 'cept'n when somebody's maid makes off with a paira diamond earrings, or some fool kid steals a car and has hisse'f a joy-ride. This-here's the biggest thing happened out this way since them 'Grove o' Doom' murders back in '33 up at the Chittenden place. Afore moh time, that one wuz, thank th' Good Lord! But now I got me plumb in the middle of all this-here crazy gray-note-an'-Invisible-Death nonsense, an' it's upta me t'cope wif. So I shore am right pleased yore here, Mister Prince; an if'n there's anythang *I* can do t'help ya, please feel free."

Nick Naldini preened his blue-black beard and mustache with a Mephistophelean leer.

"There's something you can do for *me*, Constable," husked the lanky magician with a sardonic twinkle in his eye. "And that is, explain how a couple of lawmen with your accents ended up here, right smack in the middle of the Long Island aristocracy!"

Constable Oglethorpe Gibbs grinned sheepishly.

"Yew noticed hit, too, huh, Mister Naldiny? Figger as how Redneck an' I about lost our Georgy-talkin' ways; we been up here so long, by now folks don't hardly notice."

"They don't, eh?" chuckled Nick.

"Yep. Fact is, Pappy moved north near-'bout fifty year ago, and settled down right around here, built hisse'f a good old country store ('course, this were all farm country, back then). We Gibbses jest stayed on. Redneck, here, he come up ten, twelve year ago, to he'p me out wif all the work, an' also on account of he were all alone ina world when his Pap done up an' died. Blast it all, he's done stayed ever since!"

"I guess I'm answered," Nick grinned satanically.

Zarkon cleared his throat.

"As for your offer of help, Constable, I appreciate it; let's hope your confidence in the efficacy of my aid in this case will not prove misplaced. Obviously, the first thing to do is to contact Detective Inspector Ricks of Homicide and have him check out the ownership and rental history of the red brick house to which the Grim Reaper directs Mr. Mather to deposit the stock certificates. Then you might ask him to contact Interpol and find out as much as he can about this corporation in Switzerland. Doubtless it will prove to be just another of those dummy corporate fronts the Swiss are so famous for, along with their anonymous numbered bank accounts; but it's worth checking, anyway."

"Yessir," breathed Oglethorpe Gibbs earnestly. "I'll do everthang yew say!"

"And one thing more," added Zarkon. "Find out which of Mr. Mather's servants joined his staff, say, over the last three months, and get the name of the employment service from which he hired them. Let me have that information as soon as you get it, will you? I will be staying at the Streiger estate for at least the next day or two."

They exchanged a parting handshake and Zarkon drove away. Constable Oglethorpe Gibbs looked after the expensive imported foreign limousine admiringly.

"Shore do talk nice, thet feller," he breathed. "Talks jest like one o' them acter-fellers ona teevee. Blast it, boy, hit's near about as good as readin' a book, justa lissen at thet Prince feller talk! Hoo-*eee!*"

"Shore is, Oggie," said Redford Pickett amiably.

"An' don't call me Oggie, dadrat it! Call me *Uncle* Oggie, boy, an' show yer manners! Feller'd think yew was brung up wif th' hogs."

"Shore will, Oggie. *Uncle* Oggie, thet is," said Redford Pickett agreeably.

CHAPTER 8

Dr. Grimshaw's Story

When Zarkon called Scorchy Muldoon and Ace Harrigan at their room in the Holmwood Inn and instructed them to go out to Dr. Ernest Grimshaw's office and question the physician on the results of his examination of the body of Jerred Streiger, it came as a very welcome diversion.

Since they had arrived earlier that afternoon in the small Long Island town, Ace and Scorchy had done little more than wander into bars and question people about strangers in the neighborhood. To call their inquiry fruitless would be to employ an understatement: as the burly bartender of the Kitkat Club observed in response to Scorchy's question— "There ain't been any strangers around here until *you* come, stranger."

Now that they were actually going to get out and do something, Scorchy's woeful manner vanished as if by magic. The redhead grinned all over his face, blue eyes shining; he rubbed his palms together briskly. "Ohboyohboyohboy!" he chortled. "Action at last?"

"Sure," said Ace Harrigan in a bored manner. "If you call chatting with some old geezer of a country pill-pusher 'action.'"

They got out and piled into the big sports car and tooled away from the inn. Dr. Grimshaw's office was in the Professional Building, which fronted on the town square, right opposite the courthouse. A light was still on in the clinic, so apparently Zarkon's guess that country doctors don't keep bankers' hours had been an accurate one.

Scorchy rang the bell. A voice, muffled and distracted-sounding, told him to come in. He pushed the door open and entered, with Ace Harrigan at his heels. Everything was white porcelain and stainless steel, scrubbed and sparkling and smelling of disinfectant.

"Doc Grimshaw?" inquired Scorchy.

"Be with you in a moment," murmured a voice from behind a white partition. They heard the clink and tinkle of instruments being put in a metal dish of some sort, the rush and gurgle of water. Then:

"That'll be all, Timmy. See you next week."

"Okay, Doc. Thanks a lot!"

A freckle-faced boy of ten or eleven emerged from behind the screen tenderly carrying against his chest a small, tousled puppy with a freshly-bandaged paw. He ducked out the door.

Scorchy glanced at Ace and shrugged.

"Maybe we got the vet's office by mistake," suggested the fiery-haired little boxer. He got up to go; then a white-gowned figure appeared from behind the screen and his jaw fell halfway to the floor. Even Ace Harrigan gasped and blinked.

"Who are you two birds, more of them big city reporters?" snapped an acid voice.

"*You* ain't no Dr. Ernest Grimshaw!" Scorchy protested feebly.

"Ernest*ine* Grimshaw, dammit," snarled the white-gowned physician testily. "First an' only time I get my name in the big city papers, and they spell it wrong!"

The cause of the astonishment of Scorchy Muldoon and Ace Harrigan was clearly visible in the tumbling masses of golden curls which framed the winsome, heart-shaped face of the lissom, blue-eyed girl in the white laboratory gown. As for that gown itself, I need say no more than to observe that it curved out in just the right places, and curved in at all the other places.

In short, Doctor Ernestine Grimshaw was something to write home about. Or to leave home *for*. A stunningly beautiful young woman with flashing eyes.

But with a temper. And a tongue!

She eyed the two of them contemptuously. Of the two, Ace Harrigan came rather near to being something girls dream about, with his lean, trim, athletic figure, frank open face, healthy golden tan, and crisp short curly hair. But Ernestine Grimshaw was obviously not impressed. She eyed his tan disapprovingly.

"Lacotatin superfluity," was her only comment.

As for the peppery little bantamweight, who barely came up to her armpit, she dismissed him even more sharply.

"Thyroid deficiency," she snapped. Scorchy, whose temper invariably flared at the slightest allusion to his modicum of inches, flushed scarlet and glared.

"Now, you be after mindin' yer tongue, me colleen," he growled, the brogue creeping into his tone as it did when he got temperish.

"With a Barry Fitzgerald accent, yet!" groaned the girl doctor. "Look here. It's been a long, hard day and I want nothing more than to get out of here and into someplace dark and smoky, where I can curl up with a nice dry martini. So if you two newspaper clowns will just clear out and make up your own lies for a change, instead of merely misquoting them, I'll be plenty grateful. Scoot, now. *Vamoose!*"

It was, as things turned out, Ace Harrigan who cooled tempers down and made peace all around. The crack aviator might have made a first-rate diplomat, with his natural gift for tact, had it not been that a career of crime-fighting promised more action. They dropped Ernestine Grimshaw off at her room in the boarding-house, cooled their heels on the sidewalk while she changed into something slinky, then squired her into the Cozy Oak for prime ribs and baked potatoes with sour cream, washed down with liberal doses of dry martini on the rocks.

The girl doctor turned out to be something almost, if not quite, human. At least after working hours.

"I still can't get over it," she observed around a morsel of succulent beef. "I always heard Prince Zarkon surrounded himself with some pretty sharp professional talent. But for the life of me, I can't imagine ol' Thyroid Deficiency here being able to do much of anything besides dress in ghastly taste and talk like something out of a road company production of _Abie's Irish Rose_ . . ."

Scorchy nearly choked in mid-swig on his Dr. Pepper. Ace turned a guffaw into a bad imitation of a cough: the feisty little bantamweight prided himself on his success with the ladies, and generally, when an attractive young girl hove into view during one of these adventures, he and Nick Naldini made a habit of one-upping each other for the charmer's favor. But this hard-tongued beauty, with the tumbling curls that were like sunshine spun into silk, seemed to have gotten Scorchy's number from the start.

"Aw, c'mon, Doc, lay off, willya?" moaned the Pride of the Muldoons. "We're here on business, dang it all! This is important stuff, isn't it?"

"I suppose so," the girl agreed absently. "A stroke is always important, in my book. Poor man! Richer'n Croesus, house like Buckingham Palace, and fifteen million stashed away in gilt-edged securities. And—_blooey_. One little blood clot . . . where no blood clot had any right to be."

Ace Harrigan pounced on that one. "You still haven't isolated the cause of death, then?" he asked keenly.

The girl shrugged, which did delicious things to the blond curls and the slinky dress. "Sure. A blood clot. But why the old man should have one beats me. Arteries were clean as a whistle. Nary a smidge of cholesterol from stem to stern. And you could drive a donkey-engine with a heart as tough and strong as his."

"Aren't there drugs that will cause a clot?" inquired the handsome young aviator. "Any trace of them in his bloodstream?"

The girl finished her third martini and sucked meditatively on her olive for a moment before replying.

"The answer to the first one is 'yes,' and the answer to the second one is 'no,'" she said, chewing into the olive. "I checked the old boy out. Blood, brain, heart, liver, stomach. Everywhere that something which shouldn't have been there might be, if you follow me after three martinis. Nothing. No foreign substance of any kind—and nothing that could possibly have caused the clot."

"You're sure there *was* a clot?" Ace asked. She nodded.

"Yep. Found it right where I thought I would. Just a clot— nothing odd about it. But why he developed a clot is more than I know."

Ace settled the bill and tucked the tip under the third martini glass where the waiter was certain to find it if he looked. They wandered toward the door. Ernestine Grimshaw stretched lazily, smooth creamy arms extended to the sky, and yawned, drinking in the fresh clean night air.

"What a meal! And Lou makes great martinis. Enough to make a girl G.P. feel almost human, after a day spent among the hernias, cataracts, and varicose veins of the community!" She eyed them both in a less-unfriendly manner. "You ginks ought to come prowling around more often. It's nice to have dinner bought for you; if I look another frozen food in the face, I'll gag."

"Say, howcum you were fixin' up that kid's pup, anyway?" it occurred to Scorchy Muldoon to ask.

"Why not?" yawned Ernestine Grimshaw sleepily. "We got no resident vet around here. And it sure was a cute little feller! God, I could sleep for a week . . . what great prime ribs! You two clowns come around tomorrow at quittin' time and let's do all of this over again. Questions and answers, prime ribs and martinis."

Ace grinned; there was something about this young lady he found irrepressibly amusing and delightful.

The red light was blinking on the dash. Ace unlimbered the mobile telephone unit, uh-huh'd into it a couple of times, then hung it up and snapped into action.

"Hop to it, Scorchy! The chief wants us back at Streiger's place, pronto. Something's happened, dunno what. Climb in."

"Wow! Sure. Let's go. Uh—sorry, Doc, we'd drive you home but, you know, we—uh—"

"Oh no you don't, Short, Snub-Nosed, and Funny-Lookin'. You're not dumping Ernestine Grimshaw, M.D., on a moonlit street corner with three great martinis sloshing around inside, doing weird things to the forebrain!" With a determined snort, the blond girl got in the back seat and closed the door.

"Lay on, MacDuff! And don't spare the horses," she said firmly. "You can always take me home later. I'll go with you to Streiger's place. After all, I never met a Balkan Prince before. It might turn out to be fun!"

CHAPTER 9

The Game's Afoot

They were driving from the mansion of Ogilvie Mather, on their way back to Twelve Oaks, when the alarm buzzed. Zarkon took a flat metal case out of the pocket of his gray jacket and studied the dials. His golden features maintained their normal inscrutable calm, but Nick recognized the glint of excitement in his eyes.

"Step on it, Nick. Use the siren if you have to," was all the Prince had to say. Nick sighed, his shoulders heaving histrionically.

"Sometimes this habit of keeping everything to yourself gives me a bit of a pain, chief," he complained. "What's going on? What does that signal mean?"

"It means that one of the staff at Twelve Oaks has just left the property," Zarkon said impassively. Nick glanced at him, exasperatedly.

"What about it?" he demanded.

"Maybe nothing, or maybe a lot. I was expecting this to happen, but not quite *this* soon. Can't you go any faster? What about using the siren?"

"Chief, I'm pushing this buggy all the way as it is," said Nick from between clenched teeth. "I don't need the siren, there's no traffic on these local roads at this hour. *What* signal? For the luvva Houdini, chief, what's going on?"

Zarkon looked slightly uncomfortable. He did not like to

discuss his methods, sometimes; this, apparently, was one of those times. He cleared his throat at Nick's mutinous glare.

"Did you happen to notice my behavior back at Twelve Oaks when I questioned Streiger's servants?" he asked, seemingly striving to change the subject.

"Sure," said Nick grimly. "You were democracy in action; you shook hands with everybody, even the teen-aged gardener's kid helper, and what about it? You mean there was something I missed? I thought you were just displaying 'the common touch,' *à la* Kipling, to put them all at their ease!"

Amusement gleamed briefly in Zarkon's enigmatic eyes, and was gone. He reached into his pocket and drew out a card of straight pins.

"There was a little more to it than that, Nick," he confessed. "My friendly actions were to disguise the fact that I tried to unobtrusively stick one of these pins somewhere in the clothing each of Streiger's servants wore." He showed the card to Nick, who glanced at them with a puzzled frown. Save for the fact that the heads of the pins were tiny silvery beads, instead of being flat like the heads of most straight pins, there was nothing about them that seemed remarkable to the eye.

"I don't get it, boss," he admitted. "What d'you mean, you stuck a pin in everybody's clothes?"

"You should get it, Nick," said Zarkon with just the slightest trace of a grin. "Because it was you who taught me the magicians' tricks of misdirection. While they were distracted by a significant question or a steady look or hand-gesture, I inserted one of these pins somewhere in their clothing. The cuff of a jacket, for instance; or the lapel of a coat; sometimes in the shoulder-padding . . ."

"But what *for?*" asked Nick Naldini, his voice squeaking on the last word with exasperation.

"Because the head of each pin contains a miniaturized radio-sender, each tuned to a different wave-length," said Zarkon. Nick looked blank with amazement.

"In the head of a *pin?*" he gasped. "Is it possible? A whole sending-set? Wow! Chief, I know you and Menlo have been working on techniques of superminiaturizing some gadgets for months, but that really beats all!"

"Not really a sending set," confessed Zarkon. "An energy cell like a tiny electric battery; but a cell that radiates energy in the radio frequencies. We should be able to trace the movements of any of Streiger's servants on the location-finder. I asked Doc and Menlo to bring it in the cargo chopper; they should have it set up at Streiger's by now," he added grimly. "At least, let's hope they do . . . if not, all of this has been time wasted—"

He broke off as, just at that moment, a second alarm signal joined voices with the first. Zarkon regarded the pocket set with worried eyes.

"*Now* what's up?" asked Nick bewilderedly.

"That means someone else has left the estate," Zarkon said tonelessly.

"But how do you know? Wouldn't these dang pins all be broadcasting steadily?" asked Nick querulously: radio was something beyond him. It was all the lanky ex-vaudevillian could do to change the batteries in a flashlight.

"They are all broadcasting continuously, of course," said Zarkon. "But I installed another sender at the gatehouse which blankets and neutralizes their signal while they remain on the estate. Once one of the servants leaves the property with one of my little trick pins in his clothes, he gets out from under the blanketing effect of the sender at the gate, and his signal trips an alarm in this set I've been carrying."

"I begin to get it," Nick nodded with satisfaction. "One sweet little gadget to have, chief, when you gotta house full of murder suspects. Just sit tight and wait for the guilty party to cut and run, eh?"

"That's about it," smiled Zarkon. "I'm going to put through a call to Scorchy and Ace in the Vanzetti now, and tell them to come back to Streiger's. We may need the whole team to follow these suspects, since we now have two on the move." He dialed the mobile unit in the second car and spoke to his lieutenants, who had just concluded their interview with Dr. Ernestine Grimshaw.

As soon as he hung the phone up, it rang again.

"Zarkon speaking," he said into the receiver. He listened intently to the voice at the other end, making no comment, then thanked his informant with a quiet word and hung up and sat there staring out into the night, frowning slightly, his brows creased with thought.

Nick glanced at his chief from time to time as he twirled the car furiously down the moonlit lanes, then voiced a rude snort. Zarkon looked up questioningly.

"You're doin' it again, chief," said Nick, plaintively. "For the luvva Houdini, who was that on the phone, and what's the latest?"

"It was Sherrinford," said the Ultimate Man thoughtfully.

"Okay: Streiger's butler, right? So what's the news?" Nick prodded.

Zarkon blinked, coming out of his meditation. "I'm sorry, Nick, I was busy with my thoughts. Wondering if I had lost my knack of judging people . . ."

"Why? What did Sherrinford tell you?"

"I had asked him to alert Pipkin in case anyone tried to leave the estate, for any reason. They would have to go by the gatekeeper, you understand, because there is no other exit from the estate save for the front gate, which Pipkin would have to open, since it is invariably kept locked and only he has the keys."

"Yeah, I remember all that," drawled Nick. "That's why you gave Jeeves the Butler there the phone number of the mobile unit. So what did he have to say?"

"That Pei Ling, the new gardener's boy, just rode into town on his bicycle, to get something for the gardener."

Nick shrugged, hunched over the wheel.

"Big deal!" he snorted. "So what's so suspicious about

that? You wouldn't expect the gardener to run his own errands for himself, wouldja? Not when he's got a kid workin' for him, anyway?"

"No, that's true," Zarkon said quietly. "On the other hand, Nick, I wouldn't expect anyone to go into town to buy a special brand of fertilizer for orchids—not at ten o'clock at night, at least."

Nick's mouth fell open. He blinked stupidly; after a moment, he remembered to close it.

"Must be gettin' dense in my old age," he muttered shamefacedly. "You're right, I guess. The kid's gettin' out of there, what with more and more men from Omega moving in all the time—if Doc and Menlo got there already, that is."

He pursed his lips judiciously.

"Pei Ling, eh? That's the Chinese kid, right? The one they hired just recently, isn't he? Remember you askin' Jeeves there which of the staff had only joined in the last few months; there was that little redhead, one of the maids, and the Chinese kid—"

"Yes. The boy was hired through the Herrolds Employment Bureau, but the maid was recommended by the State Employment Service," Zarkon murmured.

"Um. Kid sure was young, though; chief, you think he was really the murderer?"

"Not necessarily, but it remains a possibility. The fact that he's only a boy suggests, to my mind, that he might well have been panicked by the arrival of Doc and Menlo into so imprudent a flight. An older man would have stayed on for another week or ten days, and then quit. This way, sneaking off at night, with an excuse that is so obviously a fabrication, certainly looks suspicious."

"Um-*hmm!*" Nick nodded with a wolfish leer. "It does that! Well, about time something broke on this case. 'The game's afoot,' then, like they say in the Sherlock Holmes stories!"

"A-bicycle, anyway," said Zarkon without inflection in his

voice. Nick did a double-take; for Zarkon actually to make a joke was so rare as to be unheard of.

"I don't get it, though," the lanky magician grumbled, a moment later. "What you said back there, I mean, about wondering if you had lost your ability of judging character. Did you think Pei Ling was probably straight, then?"

"No; actually, he was the most likely suspect on the entire staff—for reasons I will give later on, when we have more time. I was referring to the second signal . . . I have a list of the frequencies of the pins I attached to each of the servants, you see, and their names written down beside each frequency. So I knew who the two were even before Sherrinford called in confirming it."

"So who was Number Two?" inquired Nick interestedly.

Zarkon looked glum. He was very seldom wrong in his estimate of a man's trustworthiness; but maybe this was one time when he *had* been taken in.

"Streiger's Hindu valet," he admitted. "Chandra Lal. He was the other man who left the house—and without any reason at all. In fact he just pushed the gatekeeper aside, grabbed a car, and drove off with Pipkin shouting after him to stop."

CHAPTER 10

Following the Trail

After his conversation with Prince Zarkon in the study at Twelve Oaks, Chandra Lal returned to his cramped little room in the servants' wing fired with a sense of mission and purpose. The Hindu valet was fiercely determined to prove himself worthy of Zarkon's trust. Entering his quarters, he donned a dark suit of Western manufacture, although retaining his turban. Hesitating at the door for a moment, he made up his mind and crossed over to his bed. From beneath the mattress Chandra Lal withdrew a long steel knife in a handsome leather sheath. This weapon he secreted about his person, then left the room.

Chandra Lal was a familiar figure about the big house, and none of the servants took any particular notice of him. The hawk-faced Hindu had always kept very much to himself, seldom mingling with the other servants to any particular extent. And, as Jerred Streiger's personal valet and bodyservant, his duties were separate and apart from those of the others who worked about the huge estate. For this reason, too, his comings and goings were unobtrusive and unnoticed.

For some time, then, Chandra Lal strolled about the property without arousing anyone's attention or curiosity. He quietly ascertained the exact location of each and every member of the staff during these seemingly-aimless perambulations, and periodically checked back upon each person to make certain the other servants were properly employed about their ordinary routine.

When the young Chinese boy, Pei Ling, headed for the front gate some while later in the day, it was therefore Chandra Lal alone who observed the fact and found it odd. Evening had fallen, all stores in town would be closed hours ago, and the tall Hindu could think of no conceivable legitimate errand on which the gardener's boy could possibly be bound at such an unlikely hour.

Suspicious though he was, Chandra Lal wished to check with the gardener first, before taking an action that might make him seem foolish in the eyes of Prince Zarkon. While young Pei Ling was still wheeling his bicycle toward the gatekeeper's cottage, the Hindu tracked down old Rumford, the gardener, to inquire on the boy's errand. He found the gardener locking up the potting shed.

"What's that you say?" demanded Rumford puzzledly. "Errand? But I didn't send th' kid on no errand; not at this-here time o' night! You crazy er sumpin, Chandra? Stores in town don't none of 'em stay open past nine. I'd hafta be drunker'n a skunk to send th' kid ina town—it's past ten awready!"

Chandra Lal said nothing, but his eyes gleamed with that same fierce light that shines in the eyes of a hunting dog when he has picked up the scent of his prey. Without a word, the tall, dark-skinned man in the immaculate turban turned on his heel and sprinted down the drive for the front gate. As he reached it, old Pipkin was just closing it. The silver-haired man regarded the Hindu with bafflement.

"Why, sure, the kid just left a minute ago—headin' that way, into town, he said. What about it—hey! You can't take that car! Get away from there, you crazy Indian!"

There was no time for explanations, no time to be wasted in fruitless conversation. With every moment that passed, the Chinese boy was speeding down the road into the night on his bicycle. To catch up with the fleeing culprit before he made good his escape, Chandra Lal required something faster than a bicycle—

And there, parked right beside the gatekeeper's cottage, was a battered old Ford pickup truck. The keys were still in the ignition. Pushing the old man aside, the Hindu sprang behind the wheel. With a cough and a grunt, the engine grumbled into life. Chandra Lal drove the old rattletrap out of the half-open gate and vanished down the road with Pipkin yelling after him, shaking an impotent fist in the air.

The night was dark and, thus far, at least, moonless. The tree-lined country lane curved and coiled its way through the impenetrable gloom. Nowhere ahead did Chandra Lal spy the glimmer of his headlights sheening off the tail-reflector of Pei Ling's bicycle. He drove with grim concentration, hunched over the wheel. It was only a short trip into town, and Chandra Lal saw no slightest trace of the fleeing boy on the way.

Of course, there were many other routes the boy might have chosen, private roads that led to neighboring estates, and many a short cut the lad might have taken without Chandra Lal's knowledge. Tooling through the streets of the town of Holmwood, which were all but deserted at this hour, Chandra Lal felt his heart sink hopelessly within his breast. Had the fleeing one in his flight already eluded his pursuer? What would the sahib think of his servant, once this failure became known? He would think that his trust had been misplaced! Chandra Lal groaned and gritted his teeth together in a grimace of desperation—

And then it was that Chandra Lal's roving eyes espied the bicycle leaning against a fence in the parking lot in front of the Holmwood railway station. He recognized the vehicle at a glance, and with a tigerish quickness the Hindu slammed on the brakes and brought his truck to a squealing, shuddering halt.

He sprang out of the cab and ran to the tracks. The train

was still there, just about to pull out of the station. Pei Ling was nowhere in sight, and Chandra Lal knew that the boy might only have abandoned his bicycle here to throw any possible pursuit off his trail. The mere fact that the bicycle was in the station lot did not prove that the boy had taken the train. For a single moment Chandra Lal hesitated in an agony of indecision. Then, trusting in Vishnu and Shiva, the loyal servant threw decision to the winds and took a wild chance. He sprinted for the train, which was already chugging underway and moving out of the station.

Springing up, the hawk-faced Hindu seized the handhold and drew himself onto the train. A startled conductor nearly jumped out of his skin when the bearded and turbaned figure with the flashing eyes materialized like an apparition out of the gloomy night.

"Hey! Gosh-a-mighty, mister, you c'd break your neck, jumping on a movin' train that way," the surprised conductor yelped. Then, grumblingly, "Dunno but what it's against the law, too, dag-nabit!"

"May I inquire as to the destination of this conveyance?" inquired Chandra Lal in the deferential manner he invariably employed when speaking to sahibs in positions of official authority, and in his best Oxford-trained English. The trainman gawped, then closed his mouth. Mumbling something about "danged furriners," the conductor admitted surlily that they were bound for Penn Station in Knickerbocker City.

"Stops at Holmwood, Herkwell, Winster, Roslyn, Hollis, and Jamaica," he said, rattling off the names of communities thoroughly unfamiliar to the Hindu valet. "How far you goin', anyway?"

Chandra Lal, of course, had no way of knowing the answer to that question, so he simply said that he would continue in passage to the terminal itself.

"Hmmph. Don't s'pose you bought yerse'f a ticket back at Holmwood station," grumbled the other. "They never do.

Dollar forty-five to Penn Station. And I *ain't* got change!"
Chandra Lal obligingly produced sufficient currency; grudgingly, the conductor handed him his ticket, after taking snippets out of it with his hole-puncher.

"Smokin' car down thet way, no smokin' up ahead,"
grumbled the other, nodding in the directions he had indicated verbally.

"This person does not imbibe of tobacco," said the Hindu
keenly. "Can the estimable officer answer one question?"

"Guess so," said the other.

"Has a young Chinese person boarded the conveyance? At
the Holmwood station?" asked Chandra Lal.

"Hmmph," grunted the conductor sourly. "Can't 'spect a
man t' see ever' last body gits on th' train! 'Sides, I ain't been
through the cars collectin' tickets yet. Hafta find yer friend
f'yourself, mister!"

Chandra Lal bowed silently and began making his way
through the cars. A few youths in faded denims, wearing
longish hair, dozed, using backpacks for pillows; obviously,
these were college boys who had spent the weekend on the
beaches of the Hamptons and were now returning to their
dorms. Besides these there were a few Negro women in print
dresses, slumped wearily in their seats—probably cleaning
women or weekend domestic help on their way home after
work. There were very few men on the train at this hour.

Chandra Lal controlled his impatience and continued to
prowl the train car by car. He was careful to scrutinize each
passenger without fail, and tried the doors of the washrooms
as he passed them.

It was going to take a while. But Chandra Lal had all
night.

Finally, just as they were pulling into the Roslyn station,
the Hindu spied his quarry. The Chinese boy was huddled in
a corner seat in front of the first car. His back was turned on
Chandra Lal, so that the Hindu could not see his face. Neither could Pei Ling see the hawk-faced Hindu, either, and

this was fortunate, for the Chinese youth would probably
have recognized the tall, turbaned man with the coffee-
colored skin and jutting nose.

Chandra Lal recognized him without difficulty from the
clothing the boy wore; but just to make certain he lingered
until the conductor came through this car, then asked him if
the boy in the front seat had boarded the train at Holmwood
station.

The conductor, a younger man than the one with whom
Chandra Lal had spoken earlier, shrugged boredly. "Can't
say, mister, unless I look at his ticket. See, there it is, stuck in
the little catch in back of his seat. When they get on, we
punch the box with their origin printed in it, and also their
destination. That way, nobody can pretend to be goin' only
one stop, and ride to the end of the line without payin' extra."

Chandra Lal nodded seriously. One lean brown hand
dipped into his trouser pocket. When it emerged, a five-dollar
bill was folded between the fingers. The young conductor
regarded the bill with alert and friendly interest.

"Would you be so kind as to examine the ticket of the
youth, and return here to inform me of his origin and destination?" murmured the Hindu.

"Yes, *sir!*" said the conductor smartly. He went down the
aisle, checking tickets casually until he came to the seat in
which Pei Ling reclined. The Chinese boy looked up quickly
as the conductor paused by his seat to glance at his ticket.

"Is anything wrong?" the boy inquired.

"Nossir, just routine," said the conductor brightly. "Hollis
station next stop." Turning about, he ambled back to where
Chandra Lal sat hunched over, ready to duck down in case
the boy looked around again. As he came to where Chandra
Lal sat, the conductor bent down and whispered in a conspir-
atorial tone: "Got on at Holmwood, sir; goin' all the way to
Penn Station."

Chandra Lal nodded silently and slipped the folded piece
of currency into the conductor's hand.

The conductor left the car. Chandra Lal settled back, keeping one keen eye fixed on the back of the Chinese youth's neck. The train clattered on through the night, swaying and rattling on clicking wheels that ate up the miles.

CHAPTER 11

The Signal Vanishes

By the time the big limousine pulled into the gravel-strewn carriage drive of Twelve Oaks and parked, Scorchy Muldoon and Ace Harrigan had already arrived, or so Zarkon and Nick Naldini deduced from the fact that their sleek red sports car was also drawn up in front of the huge Georgian red-brick mansion in which Jerred Streiger had so mysteriously died.

They got out and entered the house, to find Scorchy and Ace and a beautiful young woman with blond hair gathering in the library. The peppery little boxer introduced the blond girl as Ernestine Grimshaw and explained how the daily newspapers had incorrectly given her first name as "Ernest." Zarkon greeted her quietly.

Doc Jenkins and Menlo Parker were also in the big room, setting up the new location-finder.

"It was the only room in the house big enough," explained the little scientist, peevishly. "Outside o' the study, it's the only one with these French windows. We tried to get the unit in the front door, but it was too tight a fit. Stables and stuff out back don't have a power outlet."

Zarkon nodded and turned his attention to the large instrument. Doc Jenkins was engaged in putting up the big grid on which a very detailed block-by-block map of Knickerbocker City and outlying environs was drawn. The big dumb-looking sandy-haired man with the outsized hands

and feet grinned sheepishly at his leader and mumbled something about hoping he had everything fixed in place cor-
rectly. Zarkon swiftly examined the various dial-settings and
internal connections and announced everything was func-
tional.

Menlo Parker examined it with an unkind eye. "Hmmph!"
he snorted. "Hope the dang thing works, after all. You got a
signal already, chief?"

"Two of them," said Zarkon somberly. The shriveled little
scientist grinned nastily and began adjusting the machine.
Two blips of red light appeared on the map-grid, moving
very slowly in a westerly direction.

"Hmmph! Cussed thing works after all," said Menlo.
"What's the map say, Doc?"

The big foolish-looking man peered at it near-sightedly.
"'S between Herkwell and Winster," he said in his dull,
heavy tones. "Comin' into Winster. Seems to be stopping
there."

Ace scratched his chin reflectively. "Looks like those two
crooks are on the train," said the handsome aviator. "Both
towns are regular stops on the Long Island Railroad."

Zarkon nodded, but said nothing. He had already reached
the same conclusion himself.

"Pullin' outa Winster now, chief," said Doc Jenkins. They
watched the twin red blips slowly traverse the map of Long
Island.

Dr. Ernestine Grimshaw watched the scene with bright-eyed
fascination. She obviously comprehended nothing of what
was going on, or very little. So Scorchy Muldoon and Nick
Naldini hung around her, eager to explain. Both men had a
sharp eye for a good-looking girl, and generally the two rivals
competed for the attentions of whatever attractive young
female entered into one of their adventures.

"Big dumb-lookin' guy with the hands the size of baseball

catcher's mitts, he's Doc Jenkins," said Scorchy confidentially.

"That's correct, my dear young lady," grinned Nick Naldini in his fulsome, courtly way. "Nor is Jenkins quite the obtuse lout he looks. Unlike my diminutive associate here, he possesses a brilliant intelligence. In fact, he rejoices in the possession of one of the most remarkable brains in existence. You will have heard of those men fortunate enough to be born with an eidetic memory? A mind that never forgets any sensory impression? Well, this is indeed the case with Theophilus Jenkins. He has eyes like a camera and ears like a tape recorder, and a brain that functions like an IBM computer. He can instantly summon to mind any face he has ever seen, any voice he has ever heard, any fact he has ever read. Why, our Mr. Jenkins can recite, from memory alone, any book or magazine or newspaper he has ever scrutinized, although he read it ten, fifteen, even twenty years ago."

Ernestine Grimshaw nodded interestedly. "I've heard of such cases in medical history," the girl doctor murmured. "But it's fascinating to find one in person. I imagine his extraordinary talents make him a very valuable member of your organization . . ."

"Ah, that they do indeed, fair lady," smirked Nick Naldini. In close proximity to a pretty girl, the lanky magician became all oily voice and sleek good manners. He tweaked his waxed mustachios and preened his Mephistophelean little beard while hovering at the blond girl's side. Scorchy viewed this with smouldering suspicion; the long-standing feud between these two never waxed hotter than when they were both jostling for the favors of an attractive young woman.

"Pay no attention to Oilcan Harry here, miss," interposed the redheaded boxer. "Sure an' he's a smooth-talker! That other guy there, the skinny one who looks as if yez could snap his arms an' legs loike they wuz a couple o' dry sticks, he's after bein' Mendell Lowell Parker, the famous scientist and inventor. I kin innerduce ye, if ye loike; one o' my dearest

pals, unlike this broken-down ham actor an' third-rate vaudevillian, here!"

Stung to the quick, the magician turned furious eyes on the
grinning little Irishman.

"Lissen here, you half-witted Hibernian half-pint," he
began in a choked voice. In no time the two were squabbling
loudly. Bewilderedly, Ernestine Grimshaw turned to Ace
Harrigan, who was watching the show with a wide grin.

"Are they always like this, Mr. Harrigan?" she asked
faintly. He shrugged.

"Nearly always; especially when there's a pretty girl
around," he confessed slyly. "A couple of real ladies' men,
those two! But don't take their yelling too seriously. They're
actually the best of friends."

Sherrinford served coffee and cake, but the Omega men were
too interested in what was happening on the big map-grid to
do more than nibble a bit. The twin blips, still apparently rid-
ing the train, had now crossed the river and were entering
the city proper. As they got further and further away from
Holmwood, the signals got fainter and fainter. Finally, they
dimmed and flickered out.

"Pshaw! I suspected as much," snapped Menlo Parker
viciously. "Range was the problem all the time. I warned
you, chief, if you'll remember!"

Zarkon nodded grimly. "Yes, you were certainly right,
Menlo. The trouble is that the bead-sized energy cell is too
small to have enough range. Now I regret having you and
Doc come out here with the location-finder; if it was still set
up at Headquarters, you'd be close enough to the two men
for their movements to still be visible on the grid."

"Is it too late to move the gadget back to Headquarters,
chief?" inquired Doc Jenkins.

"Probably," said Zarkon glumly. "Or it will be by the time
we get it moved back and set up again. The energy cells only
have enough juice to keep broadcasting for about an hour

and a half. By the time we get the location-finder back home, they'll have gone dead anyway. Doc, what was the last location just before the signals faded out?"

Doc squinted at the tiny lettering on the grid and rattled off a street address. "Looked like they were both on the subway, chief, travelin' downtown—maybe to Brooklyn. Dang shame we lost 'em!"

"It is," Zarkon acknowledged. "But when I asked you to bring the set out here, I had no way of guessing the suspects would go into the city. I thought it likely their destination would be somewhere out here on the island. Ah, well. No use blaming ourselves for what can't be helped."

"So where does that leave us, chief?" asked Scorchy Muldoon.

"Without much in the way of leads to follow up on, I'm afraid," confessed the Ultimate Man impassively. "Ricks of Homicide is doing all the paperwork on this case, tracking down the corporation in Switzerland to which the Grim Reaper instructs his victims to sign over their holdings. I've no doubt this will prove to be one of those dummy corporations which exist only on paper, and whose directorship consists of false names with phoney addresses. Constable Gibbs is checking on the employment bureau from which Streiger hired Pei Ling, but that may prove a false trail to follow, too, leading nowhere . . ."

"So what d'we do now?" asked Scorchy plaintively. "Cripes, but I'm perishin' fer a little action! 'Tis been so long since I hit somebody, me fists is gittin' rusty from disuse."

"Like your brain, heh?" snickered Nick Naldini sarcastically. The little Irishman flushed scarlet, balled his fists, and fixed the lanky magician with a furious glare.

"Lissen here, you broken-down escape artist, watch yer tongue or I'll be after givin' me fists a little practice on yer horse-face!"

"You'll have to stand on a chair to reach up that far, short stuff," snarled Naldini.

"Oh, for the luvva Mike, will you two lay off it," grumped Doc Jenkins disgustedly. "Save all that pep and energy for the crooks we're after, can't you?"

"*What* crooks?" inquired Ace Harrigan practically. "We just lost 'em, didn't we? Now we're stuck here until something new breaks."

They started squabbling again. The telephone rang in the hall and Sherrinford appeared in the doorway to summon Prince Zarkon to take the call. A few moments later, the Man of Mysteries came back into the room. His features were as impassive and inscrutable as ever, but those who knew him well could discern a trace of excitement in his bearing.

"What's up, chief?" inquired Menlo Parker sharply. "You look perked up. Sumphin' new happen?"

"That was Constable Gibbs on the phone," said Zarkon imperturbably, but with the faintest echo of excitement behind his tone of voice. "Ogilvie Mather has just received another warning from the Grim Reaper."

CHAPTER 12

The Face at the Window

Constable Oglethorpe Gibbs and his nephew Redneck were already at the Mather estate when Zarkon and his men, together with Dr. Ernestine Grimshaw, pulled up in their cars. The disreputable-looking officer, if anything, looked to be in even shabbier condition than he had at their last meeting.

He pushed the brim of his stetson back from his perspiring forehead with one calloused thumb and sketched a sloppy salute when Zarkon came into the mansion. Between one thumb and forefinger he gingerly pinched a small gray envelope which bore no stamp.

"Shore ain' no rest fer th' weary t'night, Mister Prince," the peace officer said grumpily. "Two a these blastid li'l gray letters'n one night's more'n a feller kin bear!"

"When did this one arrive?" inquired Zarkon, opening it on the table in the foyer and examining it under the table lamp.

"Cain't say fer shore jest when, suh," piped Redford Pickett brightly. "Found hit in th' mailbox by th' road twenny minutes t'half a hour ago, though. Somebody jest up an' slipped hit in, I guess!"

Constable Oglethorpe Gibbs thrust his long, blue-stubbled jaw out belligerently. "Aw, hesh up, Redneck, cain't y'see my fren' th' Prince wuz talkin' t' me, not yew?"

"Shore thing, Oggie. Sorry, Oggie," said the immaculate young man with an amiable smile.

"An' don't call me 'Oggie,' call me *Uncle* Oggie, dang it!"

"Shore thing, Oggie. Uncle Oggie, thet is," replied the youth unabashedly.

"Dang kids jest don't show no respec' no more t'they elders these days," grouched the Constable. Then, spying Ernestine Grimshaw among the Omega men, the Constable took off his hat. "Dang good thing yew come along tew, Doc; mebbe yew'd best take a look at pore ol' Mister Mather. He's a mite porely."

"I don't have my bag with me," said that young lady, "but I'll see how he is. Which room is he in?" The Constable told her and Ernestine Grimshaw mounted the stairway.

"I imagine that Mr. Mather is somewhat shaken up by receipt of this second warning letter, arriving so close in time to the first?" murmured Prince Zarkon. Constable Oglethorpe Gibbs sniffed loudly, looking sorrowful.

"Shaken up ain' quite th' word fer it, Prince," said the officer. "Ol' man Mather jest about had himse'f a conniption fit when they foun' thet-thar second note! Got him laid out up in his room like he wuz at death's door. Cain't say I blame him none fer gettin' upset, though. I'd be near-'bout set back on moh heels too, wuz somebody a-sendin' me them li'l gray letters!"

"What's it say, chief?" inquired Nick Naldini, curiously. Zarkon handed him the letter without comment and he read it and passed it on to Scorchy with a low whistle. The letter read:

> *This is the second of seven warnings, Ogilvie Mather. You will receive five more, and you can never be certain just when they will arrive. But when the seventh and last is in your hands, if you still have not signed over your holdings in Magnum, your next visitor will be—*
>
> *The Grim Reaper*

"Cripes," muttered Scorchy uneasily, "he sure don't fool

around none, does he? The Grim Reaper, I mean!" He passed the note on to Ace Harrigan.

"Chief, does it strike you that the tempo of the delivery of the notes has picked up a bit?" asked Nick Naldini. "I mean, the seven notes that Jerred Streiger received were stretched out over two weeks, weren't they? Yet here Ogilvie Mather has already gotten two of them within just a few hours! I wonder if our man isn't running scared; maybe our presence on the scene is spooking him just a little."

"Perhaps," murmured Zarkon. Then, turning to Constable Oglethorpe Gibbs, Zarkon asked a question. "Constable, do you have that list of any recent additions to Mr. Mather's staff which I asked you to compile?"

"Shore do. It's right chere," said the Constable, digging a scrap of dirty paper from his trouser pocket.

"Who is the newest member of the staff?" inquired Prince Zarkon.

Constable Oglethorpe Gibbs squinted at the scrap of paper in his fist.

"Says here Charlie Wong; he's one a them chef fellers."

"Of Chinese extraction, I gather," said Zarkon.

"Shore is!"

"And did you also obtain the name of the hiring service Mr. Mather used?"

"Shore did."

"Was this Wong hired through the Herrolds Employment Bureau?" asked Zarkon.

Constable Oglethorpe Gibbs stared down at the piece of paper in his hand. His eyes stuck out of his long knobby face and deep in his throat he made a gargling sound.

"How did yew know thet?" he asked faintly.

Zarkon smiled, but said nothing.

Redford Pickett stuck his thumbs through his Sam Browne belt and stared at the Man of Mysteries.

"Yew mean this-here Chinaman is th' one what's sendin'

Mister Mather alla them threatenin' letters?" he asked, his
face incredulous.

Zarkon said nothing for a long moment. His inscrutable
features were an emotionless golden mask. Then—

"I dislike making predictions on the basis of such very
slender evidence," said the Man of Mysteries in a quiet voice.
"However, I believe it likely that the Chinese cook is our
man, as far as Ogilvie Mather's impending murder is concerned, anyway."

Constable Oglethorpe Gibbs stared at Zarkon, his eyes
round with surprise.

"Howcum yew figger he's th' feller slippin' pore Mister
Mather them threatenin' letters?" the officer demanded.

"Pure inference, I'm afraid," admitted Prince Zarkon
slowly. "I have little if any evidence wherewith to support
my allegation."

"Then howcum yew say—"

"The murderer of Jerred Streiger was a youth of Chinese
extraction," explained Zarkon, "who was also but recently
added to the staff. And he, too, was hired under the auspices
of the Herrolds Employment Bureau. I have yet to hear from
Detective Inspector Ricks on this point, but I believe I can
with safety predict that when we receive the word from Interpol in Geneva, it will be easy to demonstrate that this
employment service is one of the numerous business en-
terprises owned and operated by an international conglomerate called the Pan-Global Corporation."

Oglethorpe Gibbs scratched his knobby brow with one
horny thumbnail. "Hain't thet th' company th' Grim Reaper
tol' Ogilvie Mather t' sign over his holdin's tew?" he inquired
shrewdly.

"That is correct, Constable," Zarkon nodded. The Constable chewed on this curious item of information for a moment,
an angry glint appearing in his eyes.

"D'yew mean t'tell me, Mister Prince, that this-here employmint agency air in th' business o' slippin' hired assassins inta jobs where they kin bump off they employers?"

"I believe that this will eventually be proven in a court of law, yes," acknowledged Zarkon gravely. "And I also believe that Pulitzer Haines was murdered in exactly this fashion. If you care to question his staff, I expect you will find at least one servant of Chinese extraction was added to the staff in some capacity no more than a month before his death—said servant having since decamped mysteriously, leaving no forwarding address."

"Well, now, if thet shore don't beat all! Gol-ding it," swore Constable Oglethorpe Gibbs feelingly. "Redneck, yew git aroun' t' th' servants' quarters an' slap th' cuffs on this-here Charlie Wong!"

"Shore will, Oggie," said the strapping young deputy obligingly. Then, as a menacing gleam appeared in the Constable's eye, he added hastily: "*Uncle* Oggie, thet is! What's th' charge, Unk, jes' in case th' feller wants t' know?"

"Suspicion a murder, yew blastid simpleton!"

Before the young deputy could leave the room, Doctor Ernestine Grimshaw uttered a stifled shriek. With one shaking hand, the plucky girl pointed to the window.

Nick Naldini and Scorchy Muldoon, who had jumped nervously at her cry, came about, fists balled for action.

Zarkon was at the girl's side in one swift stride. His hand went reassuringly to cradle her elbow as she gulped, turned pale, and seemed about to faint.

"What is it?" he asked swiftly.

She gulped again, pointing at the window. Zarkon turned, alert and wary, to follow her gesture. Suddenly a flat, odd-looking pistol had appeared as if by magic in his long fingers.

"A face," the girl gulped. "Yellow . . . slant-eyed . . . and *evil*."

Just then a shot rang out, deafeningly. Zarkon staggered backward and went down as if kicked by an invisible mule. Before any of them could think or move, a second shot followed upon the first. And this time the lights went out in a shower of hot glass from the chandelier. The room was plunged into darkness.

"The chief!" bawled Scorchy in a voice filled with raw fury. "He drilled the chief!"

A dim shadowy figure hovered at the broken window for a moment. Then it was gone.

CHAPTER 13

House of Shadows

It seemed to take hours for the train to reach its destination. Despite the lateness of the hour, Chandra Lal did not permit his vigilance to relax. He did not dare to nod or doze; for if the Chinese youth crept from the train during one such doze, the hawk-faced Hindu would never be able to redeem himself in his own eyes. Prince Zarkon was depending upon him, Chandra Lal knew: he swore by all his gods that he would prove himself worthy of that trust.

The train paused briefly at Hollis, then at the huge Jamaica station. Then it passed under the river, and emerged in time to the tracks under Knickerbocker City itself.

"Penn Station, next stop," announced the conductor, strolling through the cars. Chandra Lal looked through dust-smudged windows but could discern nothing. The tunnel through which the train clanked and swayed was black as death itself, its dank gloom broken only by the eerie glimmer of blue signal lights.

As it happened, Chandra Lal had done very little travel in the great metropolis on his own. He was an almost complete stranger to Knickerbocker City, having passed only briefly through with his master, who had hired him months before during a visit to the Rajput country in India. The tall Hindu looked gloomy and sternly repressed a shiver. If the Chinese boy were to emerge into the city streets above their heads, Chandra Lal had little chance of being able to follow him unobserved and undetected. Or even of following him at all, since the hawk-faced Hindu did not in the least know his way around the metropolis.

He shrugged, muttering imprecations to his native pantheon.

The train pulled into the terminal at Pennsylvania Station. This, booming loudspeakers announced in a reverberating voice, was the end of the line.

Chandra Lal got quickly to his feet and ducked out of the car. He clung precariously to the narrow platform between the cars, peering through the glass doors to watch the movements of Pei Ling. The train ground to a squealing halt.

Pei Ling got off the train, with Chandra Lal trailing him some distance behind. The Chinese youth seemed to have no inkling of the fact that the Hindu followed almost at his heels, like a second shadow. The boy never once looked back.

The subway had a station in the lower levels of the mammoth train terminal. It is possible to go from the railroad train to a subway car without once emerging on the street. Pei Ling did so. Chandra Lal almost lost him when he was forced to pause in line long enough to buy a subway token. He made the last car in a desperate sprint and squeezed through the closing doors just as the train started up.

Pei Ling was nowhere to be seen in the car, which was all but deserted at this late hour. Chandra Lal walked through the swaying cars until he spied the Oriental boy ahead. He could not enter the car without taking the chance that the boy would look up and see him and, most likely, recognize him. So the Hindu straddled the jarring space between the cars and hung on for dear life. At every stop, as the doors swung open, Chandra Lal peered through the door window to make certain the boy was still on the train.

Finally the subway train reached a station at which Pei Ling got off. The station was deserted. Chandra Lal concealed himself behind a tall soft-drink dispensing machine until the boy had gone through the turnstile at the end of the platform, then raced for the exit. Emerging into the street, he peered first this way and then that. At length he spied the Chinese boy hurrying down a crooked, poorly-lit street. Sliding like a wraith, stealing from doorway to doorway, the tall Hindu followed.

They were at the edge of Chinatown now, in one of the poorest sections of Knickerbocker City. The buildings here were ramshackle and dilapidated, the streets narrow, dirty, and cloaked in darkness. The smell of Chinese cooking hung heavy on the still night air. Somewhere an ash can clattered and an alley cat yowled mournfully. The dirt-scummed windows seemed to peer blindly down upon Chandra Lal as the Hindu stalked his quarry through the dismal lonely ways.

Still without looking back, the boy crossed a deserted street and approached a squalid building. It was three storeys tall, with dusty plate-glass windows in front, piled high with boxes. Chinese letters in faded gilt spelled out a message upon these windows, but it was not one which Chandra Lal could read. The boy knocked on the door, paused, then knocked again. After a moment the door creaked open and the youth slid inside and vanished from sight.

Irresolutely, the Hindu hung around for a time, thinking the youth might emerge. But he did not reappear. Chandra Lal chewed on his underlip in an agony of indecision. Across the street, on the corner, was a glassed-in telephone booth, dimly illuminated by the street-lamp.

Five minutes went by; nothing happened.

Ten. Fifteen.

Finally, Chandra Lal left the dark doorway he had chosen for a place of concealment and stealthily approached the telephone booth. In one pocket he found a coin, inserted it in the slot, and dialed the number of Streiger's mansion on Long Island.

The phone rang and rang and rang. Chandra Lal held the receiver to his ear, cursing under his breath in the name of every god he knew. Finally, a surly voice answered. It was Borg, the dead millionaire's bodyguard.

"Whozzat?"

"This humble person is Chandra Lal."

"Hunh? *Who?*"

"Chandra Lal."

Borg stifled a gasp. When he spoke again, his tone was guarded.

"Chandra, huh? Where you at, pal? Ever'body been wonderin' where you had got to—"

"I have no time for idle conversation," said the Hindu swiftly. "Pass my message along to the sahib Prince—the Chinese youth whom I followed hither entered the city and has gone inside—" He recited the address, and also gave the name of the establishment, for over the door a shabby sign lettered in English gave the name of Wang Foo's Tea Shop.

Borg grunted, but repeated the message word for word.

Borg was about to question the Hindu further, when suddenly he heard a gasp, the crash of splintering glass, and what sounded like a gunshot.

"Chandra? You there, pal? Hey, what's goin' on?" he barked. There was no answer. Borg clicked the connection a couple of times. But there was nothing further.

On a street corner near a row of squalid buildings on the dingy edge of Chinatown, a telephone booth stood empty in the dim luminance of a street-lamp.

The glass door was broken, as if a gun-barrel had been thrust through the pane.

Shards of broken glass crunched underfoot. They were stained with wet redness.

The receiver dangled, swaying at the end of the cord. But the booth was empty.

Muffled in darkness, three shadowy figures slunk across the street, bearing a fourth, which hung limply in their arms. The figures entered the doorway of Wang Foo's Tea Shop. The interior of the building was thick with shadows. The dark figures mingled with the gloom of the interior and vanished from view.

CHAPTER 14

Race Against Time

A match sizzled in the darkness, clenched in the long fingers of Nick Naldini. With a quick stride, the stage magician crossed the room and touched the flame to tall tapers which stood in a ten-branched silver candelabra on the sideboard. The resultant illumination was feeble, but sufficient. Scorchy knelt to examine the body of Zarkon. The feisty little bantamweight was pale as the wax of the candles, and his hands shook.

"I'm all right, Scorchy," Zarkon gasped. The bullet had caught him in the side, just beneath the ribs. It had knocked the breath out of him for a moment, like a punch to the solar plexus. The shot would have injured the Ultimate Man had it not been for the fact that he was wearing one of his special "business suits," as he called them. This one had a very special lining to its jacket; the lining was of plates of tough, segmented plastic, akin to the plastic worn by infantrymen in flak jackets or body armor. In effect, it made a light but effective bullet-proof jacket.

Scorchy let out his breath in a whoosh of relief. In a few moments they had Zarkon on his feet. Redford Pickett and his uncle, Constable Gibbs, had raced outside the room with guns ready shortly after the burst of pistol-fire had knocked out the ceiling light. Now they returned, woeful-faced, having found no trace of the culprit. However, a swift search of the premises showed that Charlie Wong, the newly hired cook for the household of Ogilvie Mather, was nowhere to be found on the premises.

"Shore looks as how yew wuz right, Mister Prince," drawled Constable Oglethorpe Gibbs glumly. "But hit still beats me how yew cotched on to hit all so quick-like."

Zarkon, still a bit stiff and lame, was exercising the stiffness away. He smiled faintly at the Constable's question.

"A guess, nothing more, Constable," said the Nemesis of Evil. "Once I learned that the murderer of Jerred Streiger was of Chinese extraction and had been hired through the Herrolds Employment Bureau, I looked for a similar situation in the household of Ogilvie Mather. I have found that, in such cases of extortion and multiple murders, there is usually a pattern, a sequence of common factors. All you have to do is to examine the facts in the case, looking for striking similarities, and you have a good chance of spotting the pattern."

"Which reminds me, chief," Nick Naldini spoke up. "Back in the car, earlier this evening, remember you said that you already had a pretty good notion that Streiger's assassin was the Chinese kid, Pei Ling? That was before he had given himself away by getting out of Twelve Oaks so surreptitiously, with a phoney cover-story and all. Back at the time I was wonderin' how you stumbled to him so fast, but too many things were going on for me to get into it then. Remember the occasion? Mind explaining how you knew it?"

Zarkon shook his head. "To have used the Invisible Death against Jerred Streiger, the murderer had to be within fifteen feet of the victim—if I am correct as to the method of murder. There was no place within Streiger's study where the murderer could have been concealed. It seemed therefore likely that he was standing in the bushes outside of the French windows. I looked and found his footprints."

"So?" drawled the lanky magician, doubtfully. "How'd you know they were Pei Ling's footprints?"

"I didn't, until I questioned him," smiled the Prince. "But they were the prints of a person wearing very small size shoes, and Pei Ling had the smallest feet of any of the servants, including the maids. Also, the prints in the earth outside the study window were gouged deeper at the toe than at the heel, which suggested that the murderer had been standing on tiptoes. The most likely reason for him to do that would be that he was not very tall. Pei Ling is quite a short young man—just about the right height to have had to stand on tiptoes in order to use the murder weapon through the window."

"No use asking you what the murder weapon was, I suppose?" asked Nick sardonically, with a knowing grin. Zarkon looked vaguely uncomfortable.

"I'd rather not say until I am certain," he murmured. "There was, however, one further bit of evidence which suggested that the murderer was Pei Ling, the gardener's boy."

"So what was that?" inquired Nick Naldini.

Zarkon shrugged. "It was about the time of night when Jerred Streiger had the spotlights turned on which illuminate the exterior of the house. The murderer, therefore, ran considerable risk of being noticed as he stood there in the bushes. This risk, however, would be alleviated if he should turn out to be one of the gardeners. Who would most likely be pottering around in the shrubbery, if not one of the gardeners?"

"You got a point there, chief," admitted Nick Naldini.

"And the same thing goes for footprints," Zarkon added. "If Constable Gibbs here had noticed the prints of Pei Ling's shoes directly under the French windows, they could easily have been explained. They belonged to the gardener's boy. Anl the boy could have claimed they were days old, since, as Sherrinford tells me, they have had no rain in Holmwood for some time."

Constable Oglethorpe Gibbs was following this absently,

still preoccupied with the fact that Zarkon admitted he had some notion as to the murder weapon.

He scratched his long, bestubbled jaw thoughtfully, screwing up his knobby bald brow.

"Did I hear yew right back thar, Mister Prince?" he grumbled questioningly. "Dew yew know how this-here Invisible Death trick wuz worked?" His shrewd eyes were questioning, his voice hoarse with awe. The Man of Mysteries displayed a prescience beyond the Constable's experience.

Zarkon admitted that he had a pretty good idea of how it was done.

"If that shore don't beat all," swore the Constable with feeling.

Having limbered up his side to the point that the stiffness had faded, Zarkon now resumed his jacket. His expression was absent, his eyes preoccupied. He turned to Doc Jenkins.

"Something is beginning to connect in my mind," he said thoughtfully. "Two of the Grim Reaper's men we now know to be of Chinese extraction. Where there are two, there may very well be others. Doc, does the position at which Pei Ling's signal faded out suggest anything to you, in connection with this?"

The big dumb-looking man with the miracle brain scratched his sandy hair reflectively. His dull, vacuous watery-blue eyes blinked. "Edge of Chinatown!" he said slowly. "Kirsten Street, the six-hundred block. Right smack on the edge of Chinatown!"

Zarkon nodded, magnetic eyes flashing.

"I thought as much," he said.

Constable Gibbs took off his sweat-stained stetson and turned it around and around in his big hands.

"Yew don't mean t'suggest we air fightin' some sorta gang o' Chinamen?" he demanded incredulously. "Sounds like them crazy Tong wars they had down thar back in th' twenties! Thought them thar Tongs wuz all closed down, long time ago."

"It's not necessarily a Tong, Constable," said Zarkon. "And the Grim Reaper himself is probably not of Chinese extraction, but more than likely a white man. But there are Chinese criminals and gangsters, just as there are in every ethnic group."

"The last known Tong group operating in Knickerbocker City was wiped out in 1940," said Doc Jenkins, in the blank tone of voice he used when reciting from his photographic memory. "Wiped out or vanished or gone underground, whichever."

The telephone rang. Scorchy scampered out of the room to get it. In a moment, the peppery little boxer returned.

" 'S for you, chief," he piped. "Borg, back at Streiger's."

Zarkon went to take the call. A few moments later he returned with an expression of relief on his usually impassive features.

"Borg received a call from Chandra Lal," he announced.

"Holy Houdini!" cried Nick. "Red blip number two! D'you mean the crook had the gall to—"

"Chandra Lal saw Pei Ling leaving Streiger's estate and followed him earlier this evening," explained the Man of Mysteries. "I had asked him to keep his eyes and ears open, and to watch the other servants for me. I am relieved to learn that my confidence in him was not misplaced."

"So what did he say, chief?" asked Scorchy. "Where'd the China boy go?"

"To an establishment called Wang Foo's Tea Shop," said Zarkon grimly. "On Kirsten Street, in the six-hundred block. Right on the edge of Chinatown—where the signal faded out!"

"Hot dawg!" said Doc Jenkins delightedly, but somewhat inelegantly.

"Chinytown agin," grumbled Constable Oglethorpe Gibbs under his breath. "If'n thet don't beat all!"

"We had best get going," said Zarkon. "Nick, get the cars around; we'll drive back to Twelve Oaks and use the helicopter. That will take us into Knickerbocker City far more swiftly than we can drive."

"What's the col-sarned hurry, Mister Prince?" complained the Constable. "We kin use yew here to find this Charlie Wong feller."

"You don't need my assistance for that," said Zarkon, shaking his head. "That's a routine police affair. You can call in the highway patrol to lend you a hand. But Chandra Lal is in trouble. From the way his phone call broke off, the Grim Reaper's men have captured him. They will interrogate him to find out why he was following Pei Ling. And when they have learned he was trying to help me, they will doubtless kill him. We may be able to save the faithful Hindu's life," he said grimly, "but it will be a race against time!"

CHAPTER 15

The Hooded Man

Chandra Lal came gradually back to consciousness to find himself securely trussed, with his wrists bound tightly behind his back, and his feet tied together as well. Four slender Chinese in soft garments that looked for all the world like loose black silk pajamas were carrying him through dimly-lit rooms. They were piled high with boxes and crates, these rooms, and dust lay thickly upon the floors and hovered like an impalpable vapor in the air. The youths—for they all seemed very young—were nearly bent double beneath the weight of the rangy, long-legged Rajput, and they grunted with effort, their feet, thrust into soft slippers, whispering over the warped boards of the flooring.

The hawk-faced Hindu tested his bonds by slightly tensing the muscles of his forearms. As he did so a cutting pressure tightened about his throat, stopping his breath. The moment that Chandra Lal ceased exerting pressure upon his bound wrists, the strangling pressure at his throat lessened. In this manner the cunning and resourceful Hindu learned that a loop of his wrist-bonds was fastened about his throat.

It was an old Chinese trick, although Chandra Lal knew it not. If a man tied in this manner seriously attempted to free his hands, he could garrote himself. The Hindu wisely abandoned the attempt.

His movement had been slight and surreptitious, and the four Chinamen who lugged him through the dim, dusty

storerooms apparently did not realize their burden had returned to consciousness. Chandra lay in their grip, relaxed,
head lolling back, pretending that he was still unconscious.
But he kept his eyes slitted partway open so as to observe as
much of his surroundings and of the route whereby he was
being carried deeper into the building as he could.

Some of the doors wherethrough he was borne were secret
panels in the walls. One of them in particular excited the ad-
miration of Chandra Lal because of the cleverness with
which it was hidden. A stack of dusty bales taller than a man,
and piled every which way, stood against a wall. From the
looks of them, and from the dust which lay heavily upon their
upper surfaces, the pile of boxes had not been disturbed in
years, perhaps even decades.

One of the slim youths reached out, caught a projecting
edge of one box which jutted out precariously from the
others. His fingers fumbled for a moment, feeling for a secret
catch. They found it and pressed it home. A rusty click came
to the ears of Chandra Lal, loud in the silence of the stifling
room. Then, suddenly, the entire pile of bales and boxes
swung away from the wall, to reveal a hidden opening which
yawned blackly before them.

Through eyes squeezed half-shut, the Hindu saw that the
seemingly haphazard stack of boxes were actually all fitted
together, joined by nails or bolts in some cunning manner,
and obviously they were empty, from the lightness with
which they swung clear of the wall and the ease wherewith
the slender-wristed Chinese boy moved them. Their backs
were all securely fastened to the panel, which opened out
from the wall on rusty hinges.

Chandra Lal remained limp as if still out cold, but in-
wardly he grinned. He could not help being impressed at the
cleverness with which the secret door was concealed from
prying eyes. These Orientals were, he thought to himself,
every bit as cunning as the old Kali priest cult of his native

country, whose secret and forbidden temples were honeycombed with hidden doors and secret tunnels!

The youth in the lead fumbled with his sash for a moment,
drew forth a shiny new nickel-plated flashlight, and turned it
on. He directed the cone of brilliance into the black opening
in the wall. Now there could be seen a rickety flight of
wooden stairs which wound down into the unknown depths
beneath the buildings. They started downward, lugging the
bound figure between them. The last of them to step through
the secret door pulled it shut behind him and re-engaged the
locking mechanism. Had there been any eye to observe the
room they had just left, it would have seen nothing about
the room to denote that a party of men had passed through it.
The stack of boxes against the wall were piled crazily and
thick with dust, as if they had not been moved in years; dust
lay thick and undisturbed upon their upper surfaces, and
upon the floor itself. It would have taken a keen eye indeed to
note that the layers of dust were held by a thin coat of some
adhesive substance akin to glue, and the dust could not be
disturbed by anything less than the steel blade of a knife.

They bore the limp figure of Chandra Lal through a winding
maze of underground passages. From time to time, the boy in
the lead would hiss a sudden warning by drawing in the
breath between his teeth sharply. At such times, the others
would come to an abrupt halt while the leader did something
to the wooden beam directly ahead. These beams stood out
at intervals along the sides of the passages and after several
such sudden halts, Chandra Lal was able to make out what it
was that the young Chinaman did: there would be a rusty
nailhead in the beam which protruded a third of an inch from
the wood of the beam, and this nailhead the boy would press
firmly in so that it no longer obtruded. When this was done—
and then only—did the gang advance.

Chandra Lal was intrigued by this curious action, and
puzzled over it during the journey. When he finally

concluded the reason for these inexplicable acts, the blood
ran ice cold in his veins. *The underground passages were a
series of death-traps, and the Chinese boy was carefully
disarming them one by one.*

And Chandra Lal began to sweat. He wished now that he
had never made that phone call from the street corner—that
he had never apprised Prince Zarkon as to the location of the
secret hide-out in which the fleeing Pei Ling had sought ref-
uge.

For if Zarkon followed, he would be walking into a trap. A
trap laid with all the merciless cunning of the ageless Oriental . . . and it was Chandra Lal who was the bait in that trap!

At length, they brought him into a big dark room and
deposited him in a chair. Handcuffs were affixed to the back
and legs of this chair, and before the hawk-faced Hindu quite
realized what was happening, the cuffs closed with a metallic
click about his upper arms and feet.

Had he realized in time, perhaps the Rajput would have
resisted, would have somehow striven to fight or struggle,
despite the fact that his arms were still fastened securely
behind his back, and his feet tied together, and the strangling
cord still noosed about his neck. But now, with the clank of
grim finality, as the cuffs were locked about him, the moment
passed and his last chance to strive for freedom was gone.

He sat in a very uncomfortable position, wrists bound
tightly together in the small of his back, with his back and
arms pressed against the back of the chair. But still he pre-
tended unconsciousness, letting his head loll on one shoulder
as if he were still out. Wetness trickled down his brow from
where the Chinese boys had clubbed him with the butt of the
revolver. They had appeared out of nowhere while he stood
in the illuminated street-corner telephone booth. The first
inkling that Chandra Lal had that he was observed had come
when one of them wrenched the door open while a second
smashed the barrel of a revolver through the glass panel of

the enclosed booth to menace him. Then they had struck him
in the face and dragged him, limp and bleeding from a cut on
the brow, from the booth, his feet crunching through the
broken glass.

There was a muttered command in a sibilant tone, spoken
in a lisping, sing-song language which Chandra Lal did not
understand. Someone bent to crush a small glass vial in a
handkerchief under his nostrils. The sharp medicinal stench
of ammonia burnt his nasal passages. He coughed, gagged,
and permitted his head to raise groggily, peering about in a
mystified manner, as if still woozy from the blow on the head.

There was not the slightest trace of illumination in the
room. It was pitch-black as the inside of a cave. Chandra Lal
heard the whisper of slippers on the boards of the floor, as the
unseen youths stepped away from him. He peered about him
groggily, as if trying to ascertain his whereabouts.

Suddenly the lights came on, dazzlingly, blindingly. In-
stinctively, the tall Rajput squeezed his eyes shut against the
sudden glare of brilliance. When he peered forth cautiously
again, the bound man saw that the illumination came from a
bank of powerful spotlights set into the further wall.

Between the bank of spotlights and himself there stood a
man. Against the blaze of electric fire he was only a black
silhouette—a motionless shape, like a cardboard cutout. So
bright were the lights that flashed directly into the face of
Chandra Lal that the Hindu could not make out the slightest
detail of the motionless man's appearance. And, since the
other was standing, and he was sitting, the altered perspec-
tive even made it impossible for the hawk-faced Hindu to
guess at the man's height.

Squinting against the glare, the Rajput blinked at the unmoving figure. It seemed swathed in bulky robes of some
opaque material, obviously arranged so as to conceal the
build of the man's body. It even concealed the sex; for all that
Chandra Lal could ascertain, the standing figure could have
been that of a woman. It was impossible to tell.

The strangest thing about the robed figure was that its head was hidden in a hood or cowl. It lent the motionless figure an eerie, almost uncanny, look. It resembled nothing so much as the conventional representation of a ghost or spirit. Where the man's face should have been, the hood framed only blackness.

The hairs lifted along the nape of Chandra Lal's neck. The flesh crept on his forearms. His stomach knotted in a cold lump and icy tendrils of superstitious fear curled and slithered through his dazed, uncomprehending brain. *He could have sworn that the hood framed only—emptiness!*

But that was irrational and impossible, Chandra Lal told himself fiercely.

These men were only a gang of criminals! They were not specters or apparitions. They fought with guns and physical methods of coercion, not with black magic . . .

And then he remembered the Invisible Death, and his blood ran cold with uncanny dread. The Invisible Death! The death that struck through closed doors into empty rooms and killed without leaving so much as a scratch on the bodies of its helpless victims! What was that, if not devil magic?

The black jungles and secret shrines of India knew such weird magic . . . the hidden cities of Asia were home to uncanny cults of dark magicians . . . perhaps even here, beyond the great ocean, in the heart of a great Western metropolis, the age-old devil-magic of the East had crept, and found a hidden lair, and flourished, growing strong in the secret darkness!

Then the motionless figure spoke at last.

Its voice was one which he could have sworn he had never heard before. It had a hollow, echoing ring to it that was strange and unearthly. The sort of voice that might have spoken out of empty air, but which did not sound as if it had come from a human mouth or a living man.

"I am the Grim Reaper," it said.

CHAPTER 16

Inspector Ricks' Warning

Zarkon and the Omega men, with Doctor Ernestine Grimshaw, left the Beechview estate of Ogilvie Mather within minutes after receiving Chandra Lal's message. Traveling in two cars, they drove recklessly through the night to Jerred Streiger's mansion in Holmwood, and not a few of the local traffic laws but were severely bent, such was the dangerous speed at which Nick Naldini and Ace Harrigan drove the automobiles down the winding, tree-lined lanes.

In the back seat of the lead car, skinny little Menlo Parker squeezed his eyes shut and winced nervously as the former stage magician took a sharp turn on two wheels only. The frail physicist was in a vile temper anyway, since the curvaceous girl doctor was in the front seat, and Menlo's reputation as a woman-hater was unparalleled, to the point that his associates often joked amongst themselves that he had a physical allergy to skirts, soprano voices, and silk stockings.

The wild recklessness with which Nick Naldini took the curves, however, did nothing to alleviate the edgy nervousness of Menlo Parker. He squinted sourly at Scorchy Muldoon, who sat beside him in the rear seat of the vehicle.

"If I didn't know better, I'd say it was you drivin', Scorchy," the bony little scientist said peevishly.

The Pride of the Muldoons bristled by instinctive reflex at the crack. Scorchy's invariable inability to drive an automobile for more than thirty feet without hitting something, even if he had to cross the road and climb an embankment to manage it, was legend among the Omega men. His awful driving habits were all the more inexplicable, since the feisty little prize-fighter could do so many other things with such a high degree of professional skill. It was a topic on which Scorchy was inordinately sensitive; generally, it was Nick Naldini who made such cracks; seldom was he on the receiving end of such a remark from Menlo Parker.

The fighter cast a wounded look at the frail little scientist. "Not you, too, Menlo," he complained in injured tones. "Dang it all, 'tis unfair o' yez to make remarks loike that! 'Tain't *my* fault; it's the crummy cars they do be after makin'. Blasted things are made so cheap, these days, 'tis a scandal! 'S a wonder they let 'em on th' road at all, at all!"

Menlo Parker opened his thin lips to give utterance to a further stinging riposte; but just then Nick Naldini took another curve, an even sharper one, and on little more than one wheel, this time. Menlo closed his mouth with a sharp gasp and squinched his eyes shut.

"Let me know when we git there," he groaned faintly. "An' if it's the Pearly Gates, instead of Streiger's place, I'll not be surprised!"

Despite Menlo's dire prediction, it was to Twelve Oaks after all, and not the front door of Heaven, that Nick Naldini arrived. He pulled the long black car up before the gates, tires squealing in the gravel, and honked deafeningly until old Pipkin came tumbling out of the gatekeeper's house in his night-shirt, to see what all the hullabaloo was about. Grumbling and cursing, dragging his arms into the sleeves of a threadbare, snuff-colored robe, which he had hastily snatched up against the chill of dawn, the silver-haired old fellow opened the gates and let the two cars through, recognizing the Omega men in the glow of his flashlight.

They pulled the cars around the carriage-drive, parking

them in the rear of the house. There, squatting like a gigantic silvery insect from Mars, the big helicopter rested in the middle of an unused tennis court.

Zarkon and his men, with Ernestine Grimshaw in the rear, piled out and sprinted across the dewy grass for the copter. It was fueled and ready to go a few minutes later. Dawn was pale in the graying east as the vans started up with a whir and the chopper bounced lightly and springily on its undercarriage.

Inside, Doctor Ernestine Grimshaw stared about with surprise. She found leather-padded seats and a heated, soundproof cabin equipped with mobile phones, long-distance radio, and even a televisor screen. She had never seen a helicopter quite so roomy and comfortable and as noiseless as this one, as she remarked to Nick Naldini.

The ex-vaudevillian grinned in his Mephistophelean manner as he assisted the girl into one of the comfortable seats and helped her buckle into the safety harness.

"Wait until you see the *Silver Ghost* in action, my dear," he said, in the fawning and fulsome manner he habitually adopted when conversing with unattached young women of more than ordinary pulchritude. "She is able to sustain a truly remarkable velocity—can land on the proverbial dime—and has any number of other extraordinary conveniences and capabilities built in, which may surprise you! The craft was constructed for Prince Zarkon by the Hazzard Laboratories, right here on Long Island out at College Point, and incorporates a number of special design modifications which are of the chief's own invention."

By this time they had all climbed into the cabin of the *Silver Ghost,* found seats for themselves, strapped in, and were ready to lift off. Ace Harrigan, at the controls, pulled her nose into the air. Effortlessly as a leaf gliding on the wind, the big chopper floated up from the tennis court, circled the mansion of Jerred Streiger once, then drifted off to the west in the direction of the giant metropolis.

Since the cabin was perfectly soundproofed, Doctor Ernestine Grimshaw could not have ascertained one of the more remarkable features of Zarkon's flying ship. But that was the spectral silence wherewith the huge, glittering craft glided through the air. Most helicopters in use today raise an almost deafening clatter and can be heard approaching almost half a mile away. But the aptly-named *Silver Ghost* floated through the early morning sky as soundlessly as a drifting cloud. She seemed indeed like some apparition from the world of shadows as she soared through the dawn. An interconnecting sequence of fiberglass-insulated mufflers cut the noise of her rotors to a mere whisper, and the blades of the helicopter themselves were of a special flexible plastic which made hardly any noise at all as they sliced through the air.

Zarkon took out the mobile telephone receiver and dialed police headquarters in Knickerbocker City, asking for the Homicide Bureau, and then for Detective Inspector Ricks. In a few moments the crisp voice of that officer replied; he had, as it turned out, worked all night long over a murder case, and was luckily still at headquarters.

In terse, brief phrases, the Man of Mysteries explained the present circumstance.

"We have been able to trace the murderer of Jerred Streiger to a tea shop on the edge of Chinatown called Wang Foo's," the Ultimate Man explained. He was about to give the street address of the establishment, but as it turned out, he soon discovered, there was no need to elucidate. Surprise was eloquent in the police officer's voice as he responded.

"Wang Foo's, eh?" said Ricks in amazement. "Know it well—mighty unsavory reputation, the place has. Or had: it's been closed down for many a year. You quite sure that's the place you mean, Your Highness? Because I've had no reason to suspect that the gang was back in operation again!"

"I take it you are familiar with the establishment, Inspector?" said Zarkon.

Ricks' voice was grim as he made reply. "I'll say I am! Although Chinatown is not exactly my beat, these days, and things are pretty quiet down there now. Time was, though, when the joint was jumping, and we had more trouble down in that part of town than in the rest of the borough put together! That was back when the Tongs were still active, of course, and the gangs were going strong."

"Tell me what you know about Wang Foo's," Zarkon suggested quietly, cutting through the officer's excited verbiage.

"Well, for years it was the headquarters of one of the Chinatown gangs," said Ricks. "Wang Foo was a prosperous tea merchant, as far as anybody knew; but he turned out to be a crook. He's dead, years ago. But he's only part of the story. All that old part of Chinatown, you know, where the buildings are set back to back on crooked alleys, are a warren of hidden tunnels and secret passages. Wang Foo's shop was one of several entrances by which the initiate could gain entry to the lair of Choy Lown. He was an old man—nobody knew just how old—who squatted there in the secret heart of Chinatown, like a fat, wrinkled yellow spider at the center of his web. An evil legend, that was Choy Lown—a sinister patriarch, a mysterious sage! He ruled Chinatown from the shadows. His word was law to a horde of invisible minions; his secret lair was shielded by all sorts of cunning death-traps. It's said that only one man ever penetrated those secret defenses to confront Choy Lown face to face."

"Is this Choy Lown still alive?" inquired Zarkon.

"No, he was nearly a hundred back then, and that was in 1933, or thereabouts," said Ricks. "He's gone to his ancestors years ago; all that network of hidden passages, all those winding ways and secret mantraps—and the entrances to them, like Wang Foo's, and the Tai Yuan Oriental Shop, right down the street—they were abandoned years and years ago. If somebody's opened them up again, he's probably set himself up as a second Choy Lown. And that means trouble!"

"We are en route to Wang Foo's right now, by private

helicopter," said Zarkon. "Can you meet us there with a warrant? The name of the suspect in the Streiger killing is Pei Ling."

"Probably not his real name," mused Ricks. "I'll try to get a 'John Doe' warrant—*if* I can find a judge who's up and around at this hour! May take a while, Prince . . ."

"Any official objections if I try to get inside before you come, Inspector? Without a warrant, you understand. The matter is of some urgency. They have one of my men in there; a man acting as my agent, that is. He may be dead already, but I can't risk waiting for you and your boys."

"No objections from this end, Prince," said Ricks. "You hold an honorary commission in the force, anyway. But for gosh sakes, be careful! That place is crawling with deadly devices . . ."

"I will; thank you, Ricks. See you soon," acknowledged Zarkon, signing off.

The *Silver Ghost* was winging its way over the breadth of Long Island. Before another twenty minutes had elapsed, they would be soaring across the river. Dawn was gold and crimson in the east.

Zarkon sat bent over a street-map of Knickerbocker City, tracing the route to their goal. But his attention was not on the map at all. He was thinking of Chandra Lal.

The faithful Hindu had gone alone into deadly danger, acting on behalf of Zarkon and the Omega men. Loyal as one of his own men, and as reckless of danger, was Chandra Lal. Even now, the stalwart Rajput might be dead; at this very moment, he might be on the brink of death.

If the trusting Hindu came to a grim end because of his zeal to be of service to Omega, Zarkon knew he could never forgive himself . . .

CHAPTER 17

The Invisible Intruder

By now it was morning. Still the streets of the great metropolis were empty and deserted, although before long men and women would emerge from the towering apartment houses on their way to work. But as for now, the streets lay bare in the gray-gold light.

The *Silver Ghost* had crossed the breadth of Long Island and soared across the waves of the river, and now flew among the tower-tops of Knickerbocker City. Silent as a floating leaf, the big helicopter drifted through the fresh morning air on its whispering propeller blades. Directly above Fifth Avenue the glittering aircraft hovered, then pointed its nose downtown in the direction of squalid, teeming Chinatown.

Zarkon sat beside Ace Harrigan as the crack test-pilot guided the craft over the streets of the city.

"Head south, Ace, and watch for Mott Street," the Ultimate Man directed the young aviator. "It should be easy enough to find Wang Foo's Tea Shop from there. Graumann Street is in back of it, so keep your eyes peeled for the old Amalgamated Press Building on Graumann, that will be your major landmark. It's the only skyscraper in the vicinity of Chinatown, so it ought to be easy enough to spot from the air."

"Right, chief," Harrigan grinned. "Where are we going to land, once we spot Wang Foo's? I can bring the *Ghost* down

just about anywhere, like in the middle of the street. Say the
word."

"According to this map, there should be a parking lot only
a block away from Wang Foo's," said Zarkon. "Land the
chopper there and wait for Inspector Ricks to show up with
his squad."

"We could land right in front of the place, chief,"
protested Harrigan.

"No doubt; but that would give the show away," Zarkon
pointed out. "By the time we got in and found our way to the
warren of secret passages Ricks mentioned, the Grim Reaper
would have had sufficient advance warning to disperse his
gang and to dispose of Chandra Lal. There is just a slim
chance that Chandra Lal is still alive. While that chance
holds good, I am not going to risk imperiling the Hindu's life
by grounding the *Ghost* right in front of the tea shop. I am
going in alone, by the roof—"

"Chief!" groaned Scorchy Muldoon from the back of the
cabin, "what about the rest o' us? Me, I'm dyin' fer a bit o' action! Sure an' yer not gonna make th' rest o' us wait fer th'
cops t' arrive?"

Zarkon smiled grimly at the aggrieved tone of the little
prize-fighter's voice, but his determination remained un-
shaken.

"I'm going to do just that, Scorchy," he advised. "One man
may be able to get in unobserved, without triggering the
alarm. But we wouldn't stand much chance with the whole
gang of us charging the front door."

"Aw, fer th' luvva Mike!" said Scorchy, disgustedly. But he
knew his chief too well to continue fruitlessly protesting.
When Zarkon had once decided upon a plan of action, there
was little hope of persuading him to change his mind.

"Chief, I packed the equipment cases, everything but the
new location-finder," said Menlo Parker. "What are you taking in with you?"

"Just the vibrasuit and the tell-tale," said the Man of Mysteries.

"Righto! I'll get 'em out," muttered the skinny scientist. Unbuckling himself from the restraining harness, he began unloading equipment from the big cases bolted to the floor of the cabin behind the passenger seats. Doctor Ernestine Grimshaw craned about to watch him with interest and curiosity.

"There's the Amalgamated Press Building ahead now, chief," said Ace Harrigan. Zarkon nodded and told the handsome young aviator to take the copter up and to circle until he directed otherwise. Then he left his seat and began to don the gear which Menlo Parker handed to him.

The principal article of equipment consisted of a loose coverall garment fashioned from some odd glassy substance which seemed to be threaded through with metallic fibers. Zarkon climbed into this and zipped it shut, wriggling his hands and feet into the extremities of the curious garment. Doctor Ernestine Grimshaw noticed that the loose, baggy sleeves of the odd garment terminated in tight gloves, while the leg coverings ended in stretch-plastic overshoes, which fitted snugly over Zarkon's gray suede shoes. Batteries were slung about the waist of the weird-looking transparent suit and it was topped by a close-fitting hood-like affair, which Zarkon pulled over his head. Odd-appearing goggles with thick milky lenses fitted over his eyes, and about his brows he settled a curious lamp which pointed in the direction of his gaze no matter where he looked. This last item resembled the head-lamp worn by coal miners.

"What's all this about?" the lady doctor demanded of Doc Jenkins, in a mystified tone of voice.

The big pale freckled man with the outsized hands and feet explained in his dull, placid voice. "One of the chief's inventions," he grunted absently. "We call it the vibrasuit. Powered by those batteries on the belt-harness. 'S made of

some special kinda plastic, with a network of boron fiber
woven throughout. Current from th' belt-batteries runs
through the whole suit, you see, and creates an electromagnetic aura that surrounds anybody wearin' the stuff. Vibrates
in the same exact frequency of visible light—that's the octave
right smack between ultra-violet and infra-red, from four
thousand to seven thousand seven hundred angstroms—"

As the big, dumb-looking man with the miracle memory
seemed about to launch on a technical lecture on the electromagnetic spectrum, the girl cut him off with a pert query.

"Okay, okay; but what does it *do?*" she demanded.

Doc Jenkins looked grumpy: one of his main pleasures in
life was to display the astonishing collection of miscellaneous
information stored in his amazing mind, ready for instant re-
trieval. He sighed.

"Well—the vibration-field sorta 'jams' the light waves, just
as you can blank out one radio broadcast with another in the
same frequency, cancelling both."

The girl looked faintly incredulous.

"You mean it makes him *invisible?*" she cried sharply.

The big man shrugged amiably. "Just about," he said. "It's
not optically perfect yet—the chief an' Menlo are still
tinkerin' with it. But it's good enough to pass in a dimly-lit
environment."

The girl murmured something to herself, rolling her eyes.

"How come I've never heard of it?" she inquired, with just
a trace of skepticism in her tones. "An invention like that
ought to have hit every front page in the country . . ."

Doc Jenkins grinned hugely. "Well, you know, Miss, we
don't exactly like t' advertise! We c'n work a whole lot better
when the opposition don't know what kinda equipment we
can bring to bear on 'em."

"Okay, that makes sense," the girl nodded. Then another
puzzle occurred to her. "Listen, though, if this trick suit can-
cels out light-rays, how does he *see* from inside the thing?"

Menlo cackled approvingly. His frosty eyes almost held a trace of warmth as he glanced at the lady doctor.

"Not a bad question at all—for a woman," he snapped nastily. "Got some brains in her head, this one does. That headlamp the chief is wearin' projects in the ultra-violet, y'see, and those fancy goggles *see* in the same frequency. An' UV is part of the light spectrum invisible to the unaided human eye."

The girl looked dazed, but impressed. "An invisible man that sees by invisible light!" she murmured. "Wow!"

By this time Zarkon had adjusted the vibrasuit and settled its equipment into place, tightening the baggy plastic coveralls by means of small elastic straps so that it clung to his body.

"Ready to test now," he said to Menlo, his voice slightly muffled as it came through the mouth-grid. He adjusted a small flat instrument case mounted just below his left shoulder. A high-pitched whine rang through the cabin of the all-but-silent craft. Ernestine Grimshaw blinked her eyes. The figure of Zarkon faded from sight in a ghostly manner, leaving only a trace of blur on the empty air.

She squinched her eyes shut, rubbed them, and looked again. Nothing whatsoever of the Ultimate Man could be seen, save for the faint blur in mid-air. She could readily understand how, in dim lighting or a shadowy place, even that blurriness would be unnoticeable. The effect was truly uncanny.

"How's the UV set, chief? Goggles workin' okay?" inquired the frail little physicist.

"Functioning perfectly," said Zarkon's voice from empty air.

Parker reached out with a flat, stubby pistol in his hand. It was made of glassy plastic and rather resembled a child's toy water-pistol.

"I'd feel easier if you took th' gas-gun with you, chief," snapped the waspish scientist. "And here's the tell-tale."

"Very well," said the Lord of the Unknown. The plastic weapon and the small transparent hand-device both faded out of sight as soon as they entered the vibratory field which radiated from the suit. At this further display of scientific legerdemain, the blond girl repressed a gasp. Obviously, both the weapon and the instrument case were of substantially the same construction as was the suit itself.

"Ready, Ace," said Zarkon's voice. The aviator nodded cheerfully and brought the *Silver Ghost* down until it floated over the roof tops of Chinatown. Scorchy and Nick unfastened the cabin door and tossed out a flexible ladder made of nylon cord. There was no visible sign that Prince Zarkon had left the craft, although Ernestine Grimshaw strained her eyes to perceive such. But suddenly she was aware of an indescribable sensation that someone had left her side; it was as if there were some sixth sense of whose existence she had been unaware till now, that told her an invisible presence was no longer within the cabin.

The sensation was eerie and uncanny; almost, the plucky girl physician shivered at the strangeness of it all.

"Hold her steady, Ace, he's almost down," said Nick Naldini in his rusty, sepulchral voice. The aviator nodded, without looking up from the instrument panel.

Ernestine Grimshaw leaned over Doc's legs to peer out of the cabin window. From that viewpoint, she could see the rope ladder hanging beneath the *Silver Ghost*. It did not trail away behind the ship as it would ordinarily have done. Instead, it hung straight, as if weighed down by some invisible pressure.

And, even as the girl watched the incredible sight, suddenly the unseen weight left the bottom rungs of the ladder. It bounced up and trailed off, floating on the wind. Scorchy and Nick began to reel it in and then bolted the cabin door shut.

As the girl watched, one of the dust-scummed skylights on

the roof top suddenly became unlocked in an inexplicable manner. A moment later it closed itself again.

The *Silver Ghost* floated up and away from the roof top of Wang Foo's Tea Shop, leaving Zarkon alone behind, to prowl his invisible way deeper into the Grim Reaper's lair!

CHAPTER 18

The Death-Trap

Before he had penetrated very far into the maze of dimly-lit rooms, it became obvious to Prince Zarkon that the squalid old building had been abandoned for a very long time. Such pieces of furniture as still remained in the rooms on the second storey of the dilapidated structure were shrouded in old canvas tarpaulins, which were stiff with splotches of ancient paint, and whose folds were heavy with fine, impalpable dust. These rooms were airless and stifling, and had obviously not been opened in many years. The windows, which gave forth on the crooked Chinatown street, were thickly scummed with dirt, their catches rusted shut.

If the building had any inhabitants at all, Zarkon reasoned, they must reside either on the street level or in whatever storerooms or tunnels lay hidden beneath the streets of the city. The invisible figure turned to a rickety stairway and began cautiously to make its way down.

In one hand, Zarkon held the small instrument case he had referred to in the helicopter as "the tell-tale." At every step he took, the Man of Mysteries directed the sensitive antennae of this apparatus at floor, walls, and ceiling. From time to time a small red bulb winked, its glimmer invisible to any eye but his own. When this occurred, Zarkon would pause to trace the wiring of some device hidden within the walls and would adjust the vernier on the instrument case until he had managed to override the concealed device.

The tell-tale was little more than a powerful electrometer which registered the presence of any electrical device within its proximity. Such electrometers are familiar instruments, with many uses. Zarkon, however, had ingeniously combined the function of other mechanisms within the design of the small box he held; among these was the ability to detect and trace hidden wiring, and to analyze and report the frequency and intensity of an electric circuit.

Through the patient and scrupulous use of the tell-tale, Zarkon was thus enabled to discover in advance every detection device and alarm circuit he encountered on his way down to the street floor, and to disarm them, one by one. There were quite a few of them, he found, and they were cunningly hidden. But none of them, no matter how ingeniously they were rigged to detect the presence of an intruder, delayed him more than a few minutes.

He reached the street floor and searched it carefully, finding nothing of interest. Beyond the tearoom itself lay a long-abandoned kitchen filled with a rusty stove and mildewed cook pans, and beyond that he found a number of dusty and airless rooms obviously used at one time for storage, and still piled high with old crates, bales, and boxes.

Nowhere did the Lord of the Unknown find any evidence that the structure had been inhabited in recent years. Dust lay in thick layers on the warped floor-boards and the air was musty with the odors of mouldy tea and old cooking, and vitiated from being so long closed up. Searching the storage rooms at the rear of the building led Zarkon's quest to a dead end.

Again the Master of Omega unlimbered the small, flat mechanism. This time he activated a portion of its miniaturized instrumentation not previously employed in his search of the upper rooms. Now it projected a sonar-like pulse of radio waves, while he watched a row of meters. The beam of radio pulsations would inform him of any hidden cavities behind the walls.

In a few moments, the invisible man had located one such, which was concealed behind a stack of dusty crates. Examining this pile of boxes carefully, Zarkon was not surprised to see that not only were they fastened together into a rigid mass, but that this mass served to conceal what could only be a secret door. In another moment, Zarkon had the door open and found the black stairway leading down by which the limp body of Chandra Lal had been carried not very long before. Able to see in the impenetrable darkness by reason of his ultra-violet head-lamp and the ultra-violet goggles, the Lord of the Unknown began a slow and cautious descent of the hidden stair.

In a dimly-lit room whose walls were hung with sumptuous and priceless tapestries of ancient Oriental work, a robed and hooded man sat behind a magnificent inlaid desk, studying a sheaf of documents.

The chamber was decorated with a luxuriousness so extreme as to be virtually palatial. Low divans piled high with silk cushions stood along the tapestry-covered walls; low tabourets of exquisitely-carven mahogany, inlaid with ivory and mother-of-pearl, stood before these. An enormous incense burner of antique workmanship, fashioned from pure silver, hung by chains from the ceiling, leaking threads of blue smoke redolent of nard and myrrh and sandalwood.

The only source of illumination afforded this sumptuous chamber came from the eyes of a monstrous idol of Eastern craft, which reposed in a wall-niche directly behind the robed figure seated at the inlaid desk. This grotesque idol of Tibetan design, representing a squatting manlike monstrosity with innumerable heads, was fashioned from gilded brass. Each head glared with goggling eyes, grimacing with snarling, wide-lipped mouths that bristled with tusks and fangs. From each mouth an exaggerated carven tongue lolled hideously.

The many eyes of the manifold heads were fashioned from

red glass, and were illuminated from within so that they cast dim rays of ruby light in all directions.

The hooded man bent over the papers, as if subjecting them to a thoughtful scrutiny. From time to time he would reach out with one silk-gloved hand and add a notation to the margin of one of the papers with a small pen.

The room was utterly soundless, save for the slight rustling sound the hooded man made as he moved the sheaf of papers, the occasional scratching of the pen as he added a note to one of the documents, and the almost inaudible hiss and sizzle of the incense burning within the hanging silver lamp.

Quite suddenly, one of the dim rays of scarlet radiance began to flicker on and off. It was as if something had interfered with the source of hidden luminance. The hooded man turned to study the grimacing, many-headed idol. He noted in particular *which* of the dim red rays was flickering in so curious a manner.

Then he spoke aloud, in a soft but penetrating voice.

"Chu Ming."

A fold of gorgeous tapestry moved aside, revealing a tall narrow doorway in which stood a tall, lean Eurasian with slant green eyes and a shaven skull. Clothed only in a loincloth of scarlet crimson silk, he was nearly naked, his sallow torso an imposing mass of writhing muscle. He saluted the hooded man in a humble manner by pressing his hands together before his heart and bowing over them. As he did so, presenting the edge of his hands before him, it could be seen that they were peculiarly deformed. One continuous ridge of hard callus ran from the base of his wrist up the sides of his hands to the tip of the little finger. Doubtless many hours of karate practice had been required to create so grim a metamorphosis: those hands had been transformed by countless hours of toil into lethal weapons.

"Yes, Master?" responded the yellow man in a hissing and sibilant attempt at English.

"An uninvited stranger is approaching by Tunnel Four," said the hooded one. "Take him alive if you can."

The other bowed again and vanished into the dark doorway. His disappearance was so swiftly accomplished, and in so soundless a manner, as to seem almost magical. One moment the naked muscular yellow man was there—and the next moment he had vanished into the blackness.

The tapestry fell back into place, once again concealing the narrow black opening in the wall.

The hooded man returned to his study of the papers upon his desk.

The red eye of the hideous idol continued its silent signal.

Zarkon had traversed the length of the tunnel without thus far triggering an alarm. But there were other electronic wards which the Grim Reaper had installed to watch over the avenues which led to his secret lair.

Among these were the cunningly-concealed lenses of hidden televisors. These Zarkon had not bothered to disengage, since the electromagnetic aura of force radiated by his vibrasuit would render him invisible to any watching eye, and would even fool the hidden cameras his tell-tale had detected.

But he had at last triggered one of the secret alarms wherewith the network of subterranean tunnels was kept under continuous scrutiny.

The instrument which the invisible Zarkon bore ever in his hand could only detect and trace installations of an electronic nature. However subtly concealed, the current in the wiring of these alarm-systems could easily be located and circumvented by Zarkon's tell-tale.

But the alarm he had finally triggered into action, however, was of a totally-different nature. It was a simple, heat-sensitive solenoid which could detect even the warmth given off by a clothed human body. The reaction within the

solenoid was purely a chemical one, and thus remained unde-
tectable by Zarkon's apparatus.

The invisible man had been traversing the tunnel beneath
Wang Foo's Tea Shop by slow and cautious stages. Every
seven or eight feet the Lord of the Unknown was forced to
pause while he traced and over-rode a detector which, if not
attended to in the proper manner, would trigger one of the
death-traps wherewith the tunnel was heavily mined. It was
slow work, and could not be hurried.

Zarkon was engaged in defusing the ninth of these which
he had so far encountered, when Chu Ming came upon him.
This particular trap was in the floor of the tunnel—a pit
whose floor was lined with sharp pointed wooden stakes. The
Ultimate Man had been testing electrical signals. He had already found the proper impulse which opened the trap—it
yawned blackly before his feet—and was attempting to find
the signal that closed and locked it, when the yellow man appeared as if from thin air.

The Eurasian peered about, unable to see the man he had
been sent to kill. But even though he could not find him with
his eyes, Chu Ming knew that he was there—there by the
edge of the trap.

Chu Ming had been raised in the jungles of Burma. He had
been trained from the cradle as a hunter of tigers, and of
men. The jungle aisles are black as death; little daylight
penetrates the roof of intertangled boughs overhead. For this
reason, Burmese jungle-hunters, such as Chu Ming, are
trained so as to develop their sense of smell.

Thus it was that when Chu Ming came through the secret
door in the side of the tunnel, and faced the yawning pit of
spikes, while he could not see the invisible man before him,
he could *smell* that someone was there. He smelled a plastic
garment, elastic webbing, hot batteries; and, behind these,
he sensed the characteristic odor of human flesh.

So acute was the olfactory sense of the karate killer, that he
knew exactly where Zarkon stood by the edge of the pit.

His features distorted in a bestial snarl, the yellow-skinned giant sprang like a leopard upon the unseen figure by the open pit. For a moment they grappled together—the naked yellow man seemingly in battle with the empty air!

Then, his arms closing with crushing pressure about his unseen opponent, Chu Ming enveloped the invisible man in his terrible grip.

Locked together in silent combat, they swayed at the brink of the pit—

Then fell into it. And the sharp spikes sprang up to greet them!

CHAPTER 19

The Body in the Pit

Ace had landed the giant helicopter in the empty parking lot on the outskirts of Chinatown as the Lord of the Unknown had directed him to do. Then the five Omega men, with Ernestine Grimshaw tagging along behind, had piled out of the sleek supercraft and prepared for the assault on the Grim Reaper's stronghold. They unholstered and checked their weapons, odd-looking pistols of some light, molded plastic, that seemed as flimsy and ineffectual as children's toys.

Actually, these weapons were remarkably powerful and potent, when used with unerring accuracy. Fired by compression, they employed bullets of hard rubber rather than of steel-jacketed lead. It was Zarkon's desire, in such cases, to disable and eliminate opposing gangs, rather than to kill or cripple them. A dead man cannot be brought to the bar of justice for judgment, and can therefore make no retribution for his crimes against civilization. Neither can he serve as a source of needed information or evidence, or give testimony against his bosses. For such reasons, to say nothing of purely humanitarian scruples, Zarkon used these so-called "mercy-guns" when a shoot-out was impending.

The hard rubber bullets, when fired against nerve centers or vulnerable places such as the hinge of the jaw, the center of the forehead, or the nape of the neck, could down an enemy without killing him. The Omega men sometimes grumbled about this trace of "squeamishness" in their leader. To such as Nick and Scorchy, the only good foe is one who is permanently out of action. Still, experience had taught them that the mercy-guns—when fired with the unerring accuracy in which Zarkon had schooled his men—proved remarkably effective in rendering a gangster *hors de combat*.

Having made certain that their weapons were in fighting trim, Zarkon's lieutenants next donned protective body-armor of molded plastic similar to the flak-jackets worn by modern infantry. This was only prudent, since the crooks they would shortly be going up against had no such Zarkonian scruples, and would be throwing hot lead at them. Unlimbering gas grenades and powerful flash-bombs, the Omega men were ready for the assault. They now awaited only the arrival of the authorities to charge the Grim Reaper's hideout. As soon as Detective Inspector Ricks arrived, with a combat-ready squad of Knickerbocker City's Finest, the battle would begin.

One minor annoyance was Doctor Ernestine Grimshaw. The attractive blond girl flatly refused to be left behind in safety. Her argument was that she had been in on this case from the start, and now that the curtain was about to rise on the last act of the drama, she highly resented suggestions that she remain in the *Silver Ghost*.

"Oh no, you don't," said the young lady with firm determination, as Scorchy Muldoon and Nick Naldini strove vainly to convince her to stay in the parking lot. "You clowns are not going to talk *me* into staying behind! Why, I never had so much fun in my life! You're not going to get me to miss all the excitement—I want to find out who the Grim Reaper is, too!"

"But, Doc, lissen—" protested Scorchy Muldoon.

The blond girl shook her head adamantly.

"Not on your tintype, Charley!" she snapped. "Cut the chatter and let's get to it. Quit yakking—you're not gonna change *my* mind, so slip me one of those trick guns of yours and hand me one of those bullet-proof Mae Wests you guys use, and let's hop to it! Don't worry, Thyroid, I'll stay behind and let you bozos go in first; but I'm not going to miss the big scene, no matter what."

Scorchy stammered helplessly, flushing with fury at the repetition of the lady doctor's disparaging pet name for him, which he resented as he always resented allusions to his height, or lack of same. But in the face of such determination his protests were futile.

Exchanging a helpless shrug with Nick Naldini, Scorchy gave the girl a set of the body-armor and showed her how to use one of the mercy-guns.

Viewing the brief confrontation with a fierce sniff, skinny old Menlo Parker rolled his eyes heavenward.

"*Women!*" he snorted disapprovingly, in that one eloquent word summing up the age-old battle between the sexes.

They did not have to wait very much longer before Ricks arrived with two squad cars crammed with the police department's tactical assault force. The cops pulled up beside the big chopper and piled out into the parking lot. They wore much the same body-armor as Zarkon's men, together with heavy plastic face-shields and helmets and riot-guns. The men who would spearhead the attack had tear-gas grenades clipped to their body harness.

Behind them came Ricks himself, a grim-jawed, keen-eyed senior officer. He was accompanied by a second man dressed in an ordinary suit, with a lean tanned face and grizzled hair.

"You must be Inspector Ricks," said Nick Naldini smoothly. In brief words he introduced his associates; Ricks nodded a grim greeting to the men, most of whom he already knew, if only by reputation.

"Faith, an' I hope yez have th' warrant," said Scorchy, his Killarney-blue eyes bright with zest for the coming battle. "Sure an' I'd hate t' hafta wait some more!" With a good old-fashioned slug-fest in the offing, Scorchy's brogue crept into his voice, transforming it to what Nick Naldini called his "road show imitation of Barry Fitzgerald."

"Right here," said Ricks, slapping his breast-pocket. "Where's Prince Zarkon?"

"He's already gone in, over the roof tops," said Ace Harrigan. "The chief's worried about Chandra Lal—you know, Inspector, Jerred Streiger's bodyservant. He followed Pei Ling inside over an hour ago. Closer to two hours, I guess, by now. We just hope the Reaper hasn't turned the Invisible Death against him . . ."

"Well, we'll soon find out," said Ricks curtly, watching his men assemble in formation for the assault.

"Who's this?" demanded Menlo Parker, cocking a suspicious thumb at the other man.

"Val Kildare of the FBI," said Ricks. "Ever since he broke the Wu Fang murders some years back, he's been pretty much the Bureau's 'Chinatown man.' Knows as much about this part of town as anybody I could get; luckily, he's been recently assigned to the Bureau's Knickerbocker City office, so it wasn't hard to enlist his aid."

"If you'll recall, Ricks, I volunteered for this one," Kildare grinned. "I tried a few pot-shots against this place myself, back in the old days. Trying to keep Wu Fang from teaming up with Choy Lown. We all ready to go?"

The sergeant in charge of the tactical assault force signaled his men were prepared.

"Then move on in," said Ricks brusquely. "We'll forget the bull-horns this time, and take advantage of the no-knock law. Just bust on in and immobilize everyone inside. Move out!"

The armored cops left the parking lot at a trot, edged around the corner, crossed the street, and charged the front door of the dilapidated tea shop building. The lock gave with one crash of a heavily-booted foot, and the first rank was inside the building before the echoes of the shattering door had died on the early-morning air.

In the wake of the assault troops came Ricks and Kildare,

guns at the ready, with the Omega men at their side. The cops, forming a thin blue line, vanished one by one into the seemingly-deserted building. Once inside, they split into three groups, one squad clumping up the stairs to search the upper storey, the second combing the street level, while the remainder of them sought to find the cellars.

"This place is probably honeycombed with alarm systems, but we can't worry about that," growled Ricks. "Busting in like this is probably going to stampede the whole gang into flight, and this whole block is a maze of secret tunnels. What the hell . . . we'll risk letting the little fish get away, so long as we can hook the king-fish himself."

"The entrance to the secret passages is in the rear storeroom," rapped Kildare in a hard voice.

"This way, men!" Ricks bawled. The sergeant left two men to guard the front entrance with their riot guns held at the ready, while the rest of them piled into the back room. Finding the hidden door, they ripped it open with crowbars and began clumping down the rickety wooden steps.

Lights casting cones of piercing brilliance through the musty gloom, they found the black tunnel and went through it cautiously. Kildare had expected death-traps, but they encountered no difficulties along the route. They could not, of course, have known that Prince Zarkon had already been along this same route, and that he had carefully disarmed the traps one by one, as he located them by means of the tell-tale.

Suddenly the lead man stopped short, barking a gruff order. Directly before his booted feet yawned a black pit. Flashlights blazed, sending rays of brightness searching through the gloom. The sharp stakes were clearly visible by this illumination. They probed skyward, like the naked fangs of some fearsome and enormous reptile.

Repressing a shudder of revulsion, the blond girl mumbled something about not having missed all this fun for anything, but her voice was faint and trembling. Had not the trap been sprung, they would have come upon it unawares in the dark, and more than a few of the police officers would have tumbled headfirst into the death-pit.

Kildare edged forward, his flashlight beam searing through the blackness.

"Great Scott, there's a man down there," he said in a low voice.

"You sure?" demanded Ricks, crowding forward. "Confound it all, you're right! Dead as a doornail, too—one of those spikes went right through his throat, almost severing his head from his body. Can't quite see at this blasted angle—get more light down there, sergeant!"

He leaned over the brink of the pit, staring downward, his grim features suddenly pale.

"Can't make him out," he said huskily. "Is it . . . is it . . . it's not Zarkon, surely!"

At the words, Scorchy Muldoon gulped and turned white as paper, his generous sprinkling of freckles standing out with startling clarity against the unnatural pallor of his skin.

By his side, Nick Naldini's eyes narrowed and his lips compressed. A muttered oath in the sort of vile, gutter-Italian seldom heard this side of the back-alleys of Naples came hoarsely from him.

The Omega men crowded around the brink of the death-pit with their hearts in their mouths, jostling aside the tactical assault cops, while they directed the beams of their powerful lamps into the steep and narrow depths of the black pit where an unknown man had come to a ghastly end . . .

CHAPTER 20

The Kiss of Shiva

Slowly, by indeterminate stages, Chandra Lal returned to consciousness. His head felt woozy and light, as if all mentation had been sucked out of his brain, leaving it empty. This curious sensation aside, the hawk-faced Hindu felt no particular discomfort, although his bonds cramped his limbs and his extremities felt numb from long confinement.

Raising his head, he peered about him sharply, a quick sense of danger giving him the surge of adrenalin he needed to overcome the groggy, light-headed sensation he had experienced upon first awakening.

He was bound to a light cane chair in a semi-dark room with thick, luxurious carpeting and silken drapes. Save for himself, the silent chamber was devoid of occupancy. The scent of incense was heavy on the motionless air, together with a sharp medicinal reek he could not identify.

The brawny Rajput searched his memory for some notion of how he had come into this place and what had happened to him here. He remembered another room, starkly bare, and a robed and mysterious figure, faceless and hooded, which had stood between him and a bank of merciless lights. He recalled a series of questions issued to him by the robed figure, which he had staunchly refused to answer. Then the mystery man, whom he now realized was the Grim Reaper, had barked a curt order. Chinese thugs had ripped down

Chandra's jacket, had torn his sleeve away, revealing one bare arm. Then from the gloom had emerged a glittering hypodermic loaded with some colorless fluid. The needle had been thrust into his arm, and then . . . and then . . .

Chandra Lal shook his head fiercely, trying to force into his consciousness memories that were dim and vague. He could remember the bite of the needle as it went into his arm, and then it seemed to him that his brain became paralyzed by some weird force, so that he could no longer make it obey his own will. He remembered a calm, whispering voice that asked him question after question . . . he could just recall the sound of his own voice, mumbling disjointed answers from a numb brain . . . but after that he could not remember what had followed, or when he had been brought into this other room.

Chandra Lal scowled, his brows knitting ferociously. The tall Hindu was not an ignorant man, nor was he an uneducated one, although he had not been long in this country and knew little of its people or its ways. But even he was aware of the existence of certain Western drugs that could force a man to speak when he had determined upon keeping his silence, and that could persuade veracity from one who had sworn to lie. Doubtless the sinister mastermind of supercrime who was known only as the Grim Reaper had used one of these truth serums on him; and, if so, then it was equally doubtless that, helpless in the grip of the mind-numbing narcotic, Chandra Lal had told everything he knew . . .

The Rajput snarled a vicious oath in his native Hindustani. Not only had he failed the sahib Zarkon, but now he had betrayed him, as well!

His strong brown hands clenched the chair behind his back; it was of flimsy construction, and the ropes which still confined him were themselves insufficient to constrain him. Only the steel cuffs which bound him to the chair were beyond his powers. Straining every muscle in his mighty

frame, the Hindu rocked the chair back and forth until he
overbalanced it and fell over backward upon it. Wrenching
powerfully with his bound hands, he broke the light piece of
furniture apart, then kicked and struggled until he was free
of the cuffs. Although they still were locked about his feet
and wrists, they dangled empty, no longer holding him to the
chair.

Breaking apart the chair had also loosened the ropes which
bound him. The Rajput kicked and squirmed about on the
floor until the finger tips of one hand could brush against the
torn fabric of his shirt and the bare skin of his upper arm.
There, in a thin sheath of leather, slept a slim-bladed throwing knife which Chandra Lal kept ever about him, as was the
tradition of his noble Rajput ancestors.

He called the knife "Shiva," after that divinity the Hindu
priests term The Destroyer.

The Chinese thugs had searched him well, when they had
clubbed him into insensibility and dragged him from the
telephone booth. But they had not found Shiva where she
slept in her leather sheath strapped beneath the underside of
his upper arm.

Muttering a guttural prayer to the grim deity after whom
he had named the deadly blade, the rangy, long-legged Rajput fumbled for the hilt of the knife. By twisting his back into
a painful arch, he just managed to brush the tip of the hilt
with the tips of his fingers. Slowly, slowly, with agonizing
effort, he coaxed the worn steel blade forth. It came whispering from its sheath and at last his strong brown fingers curled
lovingly about the smooth wood of the hilt.

For a man of his suppleness and agility, it was not long
before the slim length of razory steel had bitten through the
ropes that bound his wrists. Then, to cut away the strangling
noose about his lean corded throat, and to free his feet, was
but the work of a moment.

The dangling steel cuffs were a noisy impediment to his
movements, so he tinkered with them, cursing over every

moment spent wasted futilely. But before long the keen blade had found the hidden catch and he was able to strip these from him, as well.

And now, at last, Chandra Lal was free!

He quickly rubbed his numb hands and feet, ignoring the poignant tingle as circulation returned to his extremities. A tigerish grin lit his swarthy, bearded features with a flash of strong white teeth.

Chandra Lal was free, and armed, and in the very heart of the Grim Reaper's secret citadel of crime.

And soon Shiva would drink the blood of the enemy. Soon the yellow men would wince and fall before the swift, murderous rapture of her deadly kiss!

The hooded form of the Grim Reaper sat alone at the great inlaid desk in the room whose walls were hung with tapestries. Behind him the many-headed idol of brass leered hideously, tusks grinning in frozen menace.

His attention was fixed on the papers spread before him on the polished surface of the desk. But he was alert and wary. He sensed a step at the hidden portal to his chamber, where he crouched like a fat and lethal spider, spinning his sinister web of death, intimidation, and fear.

He looked up as the fold of tapestry was drawn aside. He saw the narrow black doorway and the figure which stood silently within, still buried in the gloom of the lightless stair beyond, which led down to the tunnel of the death-traps.

"Well?" he rasped impatiently. "Speak, Chu Ming! Who was the intruder, why was he not visible on the hidden televisors, and what have you done with him?"

There was no answer from the motionless figure just within the doorway. Then it stepped forward into the dim radiance of the scarlet rays that probed into every corner of the silken chamber, beaming from the many eyes of the Tibetan idol.

"There has been a slight alteration in your plans, Reaper," said the man in the doorway quietly. "Chu Ming is dead, not

I. He hangs on the spikes in the death-pit, a fate you had reserved for me."

"Prince Zarkon," said the Grim Reaper slowly. "So . . . at last we meet face to face!"

The Lord of the Unknown nodded grimly. His magnificent body was still clad in the plastic invisibility-suit, but now its boron-impregnated fabric lay in rags upon his body—mute but eloquent testimony to his savage battle against the karate killer in the underground tunnel.

In one hand he held a slim, light weapon. It was the gas-gun which Menlo Parker had given him, back in the *Silver Ghost*. Its nozzle was pointed directly at the motionless figure of the seated man draped in dark cloth.

"How did you manage to dispose of Chu Ming?" asked the hooded crime-lord in his uncanny whisper. "He is a master of the martial arts . . . deeply learned in all the secret, stealthy, and lethal skills of hand-to-hand combat. I had not thought it possible for a man of the Western world to best him in physical combat . . ."

Zarkon's thoughtful, wary expression did not change.

"He may be a master of the martial arts of the Orient, as you say," murmured the Man of Mysteries. "But he had never come face to face with a master of *adhti* before."

"*Adhti?*" inquired the Grim Reaper in a husky whisper.

"A technique of nerve-fighting known only to the blue-robed sect in the lamaseries of Tibet," said Zarkon emotionlessly. "I studied there for six months in preparation for my crusade against criminals such as you. I am the only *adhti*-master ever to dwell in the West."

"I see," whispered the hooded man thoughtfully. "You are also the only man, save one, to have penetrated this far into the network of secret tunnels which was once the citadel of Choy Lown. Let me congratulate you upon so rare and difficult an achievement."

Zarkon said nothing; his keen, wary eyes observed every corner of the room, every motion made by his robed and hooded adversary. His gaze probed into the gloom that masked the hidden face of the motionless figure, but even his sharp and penetrating gaze could discern no single feature of the visage that hood concealed.

"I assume you have set yourself up as a successor to Choy Lown, if not indeed as Choy Lown risen from the tomb," he said quietly.

The other laughed, an eerie sound in the silken gloom, that chilling, whispering laughter.

"I have indeed!" chuckled the Grim Reaper. "The super-stitious Mongol mind is easily deceived by simple leger-demain. But my road was made easy for me—Choy Lown was venerated as a sage and patriarch, almost as the avatar of some sinister and enigmatic Oriental god! His followers, long scattered and dispersed, half expected his shade to rise again, reincarnated in the body of another. I did not disappoint them . . ."

"And now it has come to this," said Zarkon somberly. The nozzle of the gas-gun did not waver as much as a fraction of an inch: still was it fixed upon the motionless figure seated behind the desk, its silk-gloved hands filled with papers.

"Yes," whispered the Grim Reaper, "to this!" And he put down the papers which he held.

As he did so, the thumb of his left hand touched part of the mother-of-pearl inlay which adorned the top of the huge ma-hogany desk.

Blue fire blazed within the sill of the hidden door.

Zarkon stiffened as the electric shock tore through his nerves. His body arched as the electric current raged through it.

A moment later the Grim Reaper touched another portion of the inlay. The blue flame died in crackling sparks and the body of Prince Zarkon pitched forward and sprawled upon the thickly-carpeted floor.

The Grim Reaper rose from his chair and approached the motionless figure and prodded it with the toe of his shoe. The head of the fallen man lolled slackly to the push. The robed figure bent, pried the fingers of the unconscious man free of the trigger guard, took the gas-gun up, examined it curiously for a moment, then shrugged contemptuously, and tossed it aside upon the silken cushions of a low divan.

Then he stood over the sprawled figure of the Omega Man, his unseen face looking down at his helpless adversary.

Again, his whispering laughter stirred shivering echoes through the sumptuous chamber.

"Yes," he whispered, gloatingly. "It has indeed come to this, Prince Zarkon. But I fear you will not appreciate the point of my jest!"

For a moment or two he stood over the unconscious form of Zarkon. Then he returned to the huge mahogany desk and touched a secret signal. A moment later a slim Oriental youth appeared from behind the curtains. He bowed obsequiously, then stood with flat yellow face stolid and expressionless, awaiting the command of his master.

The Grim Reaper gestured negligently at the body on the floor.

"You have a knife," he said in his uncanny whisper. "Kill that man. Slit his throat!"

CHAPTER 21

The Grim Reaper at Bay

No slightest trace of expression disturbed the stolid placidity of the mask-like yellow face of the young killer as he received his orders from the robed man. He saluted again and entered the sumptuously-decorated chamber, his silken slippers whispering over the deep pile of the carpet.

He bent down and turned the unconscious man over on his back. The thug who did this, as it happened, was none other than Pei Ling, the Chinese boy who had slain Jerred Streiger by means of the Invisible Death. His slant eyes gleamed with cold malignant fires as he recognized the features of the unconscious man at his feet, for he knew that it had been Prince Zarkon who had identified him as the murderer of the millionaire owner of Twelve Oaks.

One slim, long-fingered yellow hand slid within his black garments. When that hand emerged again, it clenched a wicked, wavy-bladed Oriental knife known as a *kriss*.

"Kill him!" commanded the robed and hooded man.

Pei Ling bent to obey—

At that moment, one of the dim red rays that beamed from the many eyes of the Tibetan statue began to flicker. The Grim Reaper snapped his head around with a muffled cry. Whatever the code system used to identify the flickering ray, the hooded mastermind of crime knew that the front door of Wang Foo's Tea Shop had been forcibly entered.

"Of course!" the hooded figure rasped. "I should have known that where the chief jackal enters, the remainder of the pack would not be far behind!"

He strode swiftly from the room. At the doorway he turned and gestured abruptly to the killer who crouched over the unconscious body of Zarkon.

"Get it over!" he commanded harshly. And then he was gone and the fold of tapestry fell into place once again.

Pei Ling turned back to the body beside which he knelt, the wavy-bladed knife ready in his yellow hand. But now there was something different about the body. For an instant the Chinese youth did not comprehend what it was about the sprawled, unconscious form that had changed; the difference was some subtle alteration that eluded his comprehension.

Then he realized what it was.

Now the eyes of the electrocuted figure were open.

Pei Ling blinked in puzzlement. The black, probing gaze of Zarkon stared directly into his own eyes. They were fiery, intense, magnetic, those black eyes. They were awake and aware . . . but still the body sprawled, limp as a wax doll, motionless and unmoving.

Pei Ling was baffled. He knew the secret of the hidden door behind the tapestry. There were many such doors to this secret chamber, he knew, and all of them were wired to carry electricity. Pei Ling had been born and raised in this country and had attended English-language schools. Some little he knew of the white man's devil magic called electricity; but not much. He knew that a shock of sufficient voltage will stun a man into unconsciousness, while a shock of greater intensity will paralyze or even kill.

Then comprehension dawned in the subtle mind of Pei Ling. He understood what had happened. The man at his feet had suffered a powerful electrical shock. One which had rendered him unconscious for a time, but one that was not quite powerful enough to kill.

A shock, moreover, that had *paralyzed* the body of Prince Zarkon!

Doubtless, the paralysis was but of temporary duration. In time it would wear off and the Omega Man would once again regain the use of his limbs. But, for the moment, at any rate, the grim and untiring avenger, the all-powerful Nemesis of Evil, was completely helpless!

Helpless to avoid the edge of the knife which Pei Ling held in those clever yellow fingers . . . yet fully conscious of the danger which threatened to snuff out his life!

There was an innate strain of cruelty in the brain of Pei Ling, despite his youth. The helplessness of the enemy at his mercy appealed to that streak of savagery within him. His slit eyes gloated down into the mute but knowing eyes of Zarkon; he smiled a slow, cunning, cruel smile.

Slowly he reached out and set the razor-sharp edge of his knife against the throat of Zarkon.

Holding the gaze of those helpless eyes with his own gloating gaze, he began to exert pressure upon the blade. He thrust down, slowly, gently, the pressure of his hand as gentle as that of a woman's caress . . .

Or he tried to, at any rate!

For the nerves and muscles of his hand would no longer serve his will. He found, to his bewilderment, to his growing terror, that he could not move at all.

Neither could he tear his gaze away from the probing stare of those uncanny black eyes. Their magnetic force seemed to penetrate his skull and freeze the very brain within his head.

Globules of cold sweat burst out upon the contorted brow of Pei Ling. He strove with every atom of strength within him to move his hand, but he could not alter its position in the slightest. It was fixed and immobile, as if caught in the grip of a vise.

He could not wrench his eyes from the fiery magnetic gaze of the helpless man at his feet. Those black eyes seemed to swell and grow until they were like whirling ebon pools of

black fire which rose and rose to engulf his spirit. Like seeth-
ing whirlpools, they rose and rose to drag him down into
their swirling depths . . .

It was some time later when, prowling the secret corridors of
the Grim Reaper's domain, Chandra Lal found a door and
forced it open, to find the Chinese boy crouched in paralysis
over the recumbent form of Prince Zarkon.

The boy was frozen into immobility by Zarkon's powerful
hypnotic gaze. He was completely paralyzed, like a statue of
yellow stone.

With a snarl of tigerish wrath, the Hindu bent and
snatched his frozen form away from the Man of Mysteries,
and flung him into a corner like a lifeless wooden doll.

Then, crooning a wordless tune, the mighty Rajput knelt,
stripped away the ruins of the invisibility suit, and rubbed
and chafed Zarkon's limbs until the last traces of the paralysis
induced by the electric shock had worn away and the Omega
Man could move again.

Thus did Chandra Lal redeem himself in his own heart for
what he considered his failure and his betrayal of the sahib to
whom he knelt in loyalty and homage.

When Zarkon had recovered, he wrung the hand of the faithful Hindu in silent but eloquent thanks. Then he picked up
the gas-gun from where the Grim Reaper had carelessly
tossed it and went to tie up Pei Ling. His face became somber
as he bent to examine the boy and found that no bondage
would be necessary, for the boy was dead. His heart had simply stopped, not through any workings of Zarkon's hypnotic
spell, but, simply, through fear and fear alone.

Zarkon frowned, but there was nothing he could do about
it, and there was nothing he could say. It displeased him that,
even inadvertently, he had taken a life. The fact that Pei
Ling was a murderer, and had struck down his own employer
in cold blood, made no difference to Zarkon. The boy should

have lived to stand trial for his crime. But nothing could be done about that now . . .

With the loyal Rajput at his side, Zarkon went from the room and began to explore the secret citadel of the Grim Reaper. It was a network of rooms devoted to various purposes, all connected by narrow, wandering passages. One room was crammed full of radio equipment, among which was a powerful sending and receiving set of unique design; it was by means of this instrument, obviously, that the hooded mastermind of supercrime kept in touch with his agents. The radio operator, a slim, hairless Oriental of indeterminate years, turned from his instrument with a huge revolver at the ready. Zarkon laid him senseless on the floor with a thin hissing jet from his gas-gun.

Other rooms contained stockpiles of weapons, clothing, food. But many rooms were empty and long-unused.

Zarkon and Chandra Lal encountered three more Orientals fleeing down the hidden passages during their exploration of the secret fortress. Two of these Zarkon deftly felled with the gas-gun; the third Chandra Lal downed with his slender and lethal throwing-knife. His skill with the blade was amazing to watch. It virtually flew from his finger tips like a slim and deadly steel bird.

Zarkon was not pleased that Chandra Lal had killed the man, but said nothing. As for the Rajput, he grinned exultantly. Some of the self-esteem he had lost when the little yellow men had captured him so easily there in the street-corner telephone booth, he had now regained. At least one of his enemies had tasted the lethal kiss of Shiva! He wiped the slim blade carefully clean upon the black silk garments of the man he had killed, then hurried to rejoin Zarkon in his search for the Grim Reaper.

For now the tide had turned, and the hunted had become the hunter. And at last the Grim Reaper was at bay!

CHAPTER 22

The Empty Web

The sun was well up in the sky; the odors of cooking were on the air and yawning Chinese were opening up their shops and stands. The street had been cordoned off so that curious onlookers could not interfere with the police as they finished up their work.

Ricks, Kildare, and the others had searched the warren of secret passages, rooting out a few stragglers. Three of the fleeing thugs had been shot, four others seized, and Zarkon had used his gas-gun on two more. They were a sorry, bedraggled lot, as the sergeant hustled them into the ambulance and the paddy wagon Ricks had summoned to the scene.

Only six men taken, out of the whole gang! It wasn't much, for a night's work, thought Ricks to himself, sourly. Still and all, they had cleaned out a viper's nest of crime and had forced into flight none other than the Grim Reaper himself.

One man on the run alone can't get far, he argued to himself. But his arguments were not very convincing. With a grunt of weariness, he fished a crumpled pack of cigarettes from an inner pocket, stuck one in the corner of his mouth, and lit it with a common kitchen-match, which he scratched against the peeling paint of a police call-box positioned, with unconscious irony, directly before the entrance to Wang Foo's Tea Shop.

The Omega men came straggling out of the front door, followed by Doctor Ernestine Grimshaw and Chandra Lal. Zarkon was the last to emerge, and when he came out he was deep in a low conversation with Val Kildare of the FBI.

"Guess that's about it, Zarkon," growled Ricks as the Ultimate Man came over to greet him. "Six live ones and two stiffs. Pretty lousy haul, I'd say!"

Zarkon nodded, saying nothing. Kildare was scribbling something in a pocket notebook; he looked up at the Inspector's disgruntled remark.

"Don't forget that we have yet to trace all the tunnels," the Federal agent reminded the police homicide officer.

"Yeah, sure, but that'll take mine detectors and a full demolitions squad," Ricks shrugged. "Take a couple of days, most likely. And none of these thugs are going to stick around and wait for us to dig 'em out. They'll have all ducked out the other exits—the ones we don't know about yet—and'll be holed up safe and snug with friends and relatives or whatever. We'll never track 'em down, not unless the Grim Reaper's a lot dumber than I think he is, and kept a membership roster." Ricks grinned at the very idea, and Kildare chuckled briefly, but then frowned again.

"At least we can close up this rat's nest once and for all," he said. "I'd like to see this tea shop flattened by a bulldozer, and all those passages ripped out. Only then can we safely put the ghost of Choy Lown to rest."

Ricks nodded glumly. "Might be able to do just that," he grunted. "Get some of the local merchants and community leaders to petition City Hall to erase this blot on the neighborhood as a potential future menace to the Chinatown community. They're not all crooks an' thugs down here, you know! A lot of decent families and civic-minded businessmen. Just might get Urban Renewal to condemn all these closed-up buildings, and the city to pull 'em down . . ."

A squad car full of fingerprint technicians and electronics experts came through the police cordon and pulled up across the street. Men got out with cases of equipment and started up the steps. The entire place would be searched from top to bottom, thoroughly and scrupulously, dusted for fingerprints, and checked out by police experts. Ricks went over to talk to the officer in charge of the technical squad.

Zarkon went to where his men were grouped, followed by Chandra Lal. Scorchy Muldoon was grumbling; the feisty little prize-fighter looked grumpy and dispirited.

"Faith, an' I wuz after hopin' fer sumthin' a little more lively than a tea-party," grouched the diminutive redhead.

Nick Naldini grinned nastily, but his heart wasn't really in it. "Small Change here was gripin' about there not bein' enough heads to crack together, chief!" chuckled the lanky ex-magician in his hoarse, sepulchral voice. "I was just telling him not to be such a poor sport; after all, it isn't every day we get to poke around into a real opium-den type joint like that one. Enough fancy stuff in there to keep half a dozen Third Avenue antique dealers in business for a month, at least!"

Menlo Parker snorted—which was the waspish little scientist's equivalent of a laugh. "Yeah! What a spooky place! I kept expecting th' Ghost o' Christmas Past to come popping out of a secret panel any time."

Nick yawned a jaw-cracking yawn and rubbed the long, sensitive fingers of one hand over sallow, blue-stubbled cheeks.

"So what's next on the agenda, chief? Any leads to follow up? If not, boy, could I do with a week's sleep—it sure has been a long, busy night!"

"Not much in the way of leads," Zarkon admitted somberly, "unless the technical squad turns up something. But I doubt they will. Our man is devilishly cunning, and will have covered his traces every step of the way."

"What about all that electronics gear back in there, chief," inquired Doc Jenkins in his heavy, phlegmatic voice. "All those television cameras and body-proximity alarms and other assorted junk. Any chance of tracing that stuff back to a purchaser?"

"G'wan," mumbled Menlo Parker, muffling a yawn of his own. "You can pick up that kind of stuff in a good hardware store these days! And the rest of it you can find in the storefront bins along Radio Row," he snapped, referring to a street in downtown Knickerbocker City where radio and TV and stereo parts were retailed for home gadgeteers.

Scorchy rubbed red-rimmed eyes blearily.

"Cripes, I could do with a bit of shut-eye, meself," he complained. Doctor Ernestine Grimshaw flashed him a grin.

"That's the very first time since I met you clowns," the blond girl laughed, "that you and Daddy Long-Legs here ever agreed on anything. Better watch out, Vest Pocket, or you'll be buddies before you know it."

The Omega men chuckled while Scorchy flushed and Nick Naldini gave the grinning girl an injured look. The lanky magician was about to make a wise-crack in rebuttal when Ace Harrigan touched his arm to silence him.

"Aw, c'mon, we're all too sleepy to hear you two jaw at each other," the young aviator said. "You, too, Miss—don't encourage 'em, for the love of gosh."

"Encourage them, is it?" scoffed the lady doctor. "I don't get the feeling they need any encouragement to mix it up. If Pint Size here can't find any slant-eyes to wade into, he can always pick a squabble with his pal!"

"All kiddin' aside, what about it, chief? Where do we go from here?" asked Harrigan, turning to Zarkon.

The Lord of the Unknown said nothing for a moment. Then he smiled.

"I think the best thing to do is just that—get back to Headquarters and get cleaned up, get some hot food inside of us all, and then catch up on our sleep," he said. "We seem to have run this thing into a wall, and until something new turns up there doesn't seem to be anything else to do. We'll take the chopper back home—"

"Hey, what about me?" demanded Doctor Ernestine Grimshaw. "You're not just gonna leave me standing here on a street corner in the middle of Chinatown, are you?"

Zarkon shrugged. "We can offer you accommodations at our headquarters, if you like," said the Ultimate Man. "Or would you prefer it if we put you up at a hotel?"

"Anything, so long as it's got a bed and a kitchen," replied the blond girl, with a small, ladylike yawn.

Returning to the parking lot, they climbed aboard the *Silver Ghost;* with Ace Harrigan at the controls again, the craft rose on whirling blades, soared into the noontime sky, and flew north and west across the streets of Knickerbocker City.

Ace brought the big craft down on a certain area of the roof of the block-long complex of building-fronts that housed the Omega men. At his coded signal the roof area opened up huge folding doors to disclose a capacious hangar for the craft. The helicopter parked, the roof closed again above their heads. Ernestine Grimshaw said nothing, but from the expression on her face, the attractive female physician was quite impressed.

They piled out, unloaded most of the equipment cases into steel lockers which lined the walls of the hangar, then descended to the living area of the building. Thick Oriental carpets lay underfoot. Glass-fronted mahogany bookshelves marched around the walls, bearing rank on rank of impressive volumes; this private library ranged all the way from scientific reference works to rare first editions. Here and there, where the oak-paneled walls were unencumbered by the library shelves, superb oil paintings by modern masters glowed richly in the subdued lighting.

"You boys do yourselves right good," observed Ernestine Grimshaw tartly, examining a valuable portrait by Van Gogh set in an ornate gilded frame. The worth of the painting represented the sum total of her income for the next ten years. "Crime may not pay, as the saying goes; but it sure looks like crime-fighting does!"

Scorchy shrugged, grinned, and smothered a yawn, too bone-weary to bother explaining that the grateful democratic government of Novenia yearly paid three million dollars in gold into a Swiss bank account in the name of Prince Zarkon, as royalties for his patents on the rhombium refining process he had invented, and that this was the source of the wealth which backed the Omega organization. Zarkon made it his practice never to accept a dime from any of his clients, save in those cases where they were men or women of considerable wealth, in which situation he suggested they donate his fee to cancer research or some similarly worthy charitable cause.

Scorchy started for the fully-equipped modern kitchen to rustle up some chow, but Chandra Lal interposed himself between the little Irishman and the door.

"If the sahib Scorchy will permit me," said the tall Hindu with dignity. He vanished into the kitchen, from whence in a surprisingly short time there came the appetizing odors of ham and eggs, buttered toast, and fresh-perked coffee. Although hardly able to keep their eyes open, they feasted grandly on the largest and most delicious late breakfast any of them could recall from recent memory.

"Cripes, Chandra, ol' pal," sighed Scorchy, replete with good food. "You sure do lay out a good feed! Five kinds o' jam an' marmalade, yet! That oughta win you a pal in ol' Doc, here."

The big man grinned sheepishly and shuffled his size fifteens embarrassedly. He was famous among his colleagues for his sweet tooth, and was rarely without a half-dozen candy bars, which he secreted about his person, distributed in several different pockets, in case hunger struck.

They all complimented Chandra Lal on his cooking, then trooped off to their quarters for some shut-eye. Doctor Ernestine Grimshaw was given her pick of several unused guest rooms, and picked the one with the largest and softest-looking bed. Chandra Lal chose a small and Spartanly-decorated cubicle off the main laboratory, where a narrow Army cot was laid out. Zarkon sometimes snatched a few hours' sleep there, amidst a series of experiments. The tall Rajput claimed he desired no more luxurious accommodations.

And they slept, all of them, weary from the long night and the exhaustive morning of battle and adventure. If they dreamed at all, it was of a shadowy, hooded figure in dark robes whose faceless visage leered and laughed at them from the shadows.

For the Grim Reaper was still at large. Although they had broken into the secret lair where he squatted like an immense spider at the center of a far-flung network of villainy, the spider had eluded them, and the web was empty.

CHAPTER 23

The Noose Tightens

It was early afternoon before Ace, Nick, Scorchy, Doc, and Menlo began to stir about. When they did, they found Prince Zarkon already up and dressed. The Ultimate Man was in the living room area, in fact, conversing with someone on the telephone and taking notes on a yellow pad with a felt-tipped pen.

Scorchy shuffled into the room clad mostly in a patched and faded old bathrobe of such virulent hues it is to be doubted if the garment could find service elsewhere, even as a horse blanket. Yawning hugely, and scratching his tousled red curls, the little Irishman vanished into the kitchen and came out with a steaming mug of coffee clenched in one hand to find Zarkon hanging up the receiver.

"What's up?" he inquired, downing a hefty gulp of the brew. "Anything new?"

"Just some detail-work," admitted Zarkon quietly. "I had initiated several lines of inquiry through Inspector Ricks, Constable Gibbs, and other agencies. Interpol has been trying to figure out who, if anyone, actually owns that holding company in Switzerland—"

"Y'mean the one the Grim Reaper wanted his victims to sign over all their stocks to, huh?"

"That's the one."

A tall, lean figure appeared in the doorway. It was Nick

Naldini, looking comparatively fresh in crimson silk lounging pajamas and a black velvet smoking-jacket.

"Thought I heard voices," commented the ex-vaudevillian. "You guys leave any coffee in the pot?"

"There's plenty on the stove," Scorchy said with an offhand wave. Then, turning back to Zarkon: "Any more leads on the case, chief? Danged thing just can't peter out like that! Ricks come up with anything yet? How about that millionaire—Ogilvie Mather—any more threatening notes?"

"Nothing, from all fronts," admitted Zarkon a trifle grimly. "To such an extent that I am beginning to wonder if perhaps the Grim Reaper is not even more clever than I had estimated him to be."

"How d'ya figger that?" scowled Scorchy.

"Simply that the smartest thing he could do, right now, is to pull in his horns and sit tight and do absolutely nothing. We don't have any real leads to follow up—oh, I have a few suspicions of my own, but no real evidence that indicates a direct line of inquiry to pursue. If our adversary was cunning enough, he would completely terminate all activities and just wait us out, knowing that sooner or later something would arise and we would be off on a new case . . ."

Scorchy opened his mouth to growl some comment on that thought, when the telephone rang again. Zarkon picked it up and murmured a greeting, listened thoughtfully for a moment or two, then hung up. Almost immediately it rang again; while Zarkon was talking with the second caller, Scorchy went shuffling back into the kitchen to replenish the piping hot supply of strong black coffee in his mug.

Before long they were all up and around and reasonably *compos mentis*. Washed, shaved, dressed, they sat around feeling rather like weekend guests invited for tennis who find themselves marooned inside due to a thunderstorm. There was nothing much to do, and nowhere to go. The case had dwindled away into a stalemate of sorts. It was very discomforting.

Zarkon hung up on his last phone conversation and came over to where they sat. Something about his manner made them prick their ears.

"Something's up, isn't it, chief?" drawled Nick Naldini, waving his long cigarette holder lazily.

"Well, there's something to do, at any rate," admitted Zarkon. "That was Sherrinford on the line—"

"Sherrinford?" repeated Ernestine Grimshaw, knitting her brows perplexedly. "Oh yeah, old man Streiger's butler: I remember him now."

"And what did Jeeves want?" inquired Nick.

"The funeral of Jerred Streiger is this afternoon," said Zarkon. "It will be followed by the official reading of the will at Twelve Oaks. Sherrinford thought I might wish to know . . ."

"So, what are we gonna do, drive out there, chief?" asked Scorchy. "I'm rarin' t'go somewhere, do sumthin, but . . . I dunno . . . funerals ain't in my line. 'Sides, 'tisn't like we actually knew the old guy—"

"Oh, what the heck, let's go!" snapped Menlo Parker irritably. "We have to return to Twelve Oaks sooner or later, if only to pack up the new location-finder and bring it back with us!"

"And we should take Miss Grimshaw home," added Nick Naldini gallantly.

"Yes, I believe we will," said Zarkon. "I would like to hear the provisions of the will, at any rate, if only to see that they match what Seaton intimated they would be."

"Who's this Seaton?" demanded Scorchy bluntly.

"Josiah Seaton; Streiger's attorney."

"Oh. Well, let's go, then. But, chief, c'nt we skip the funeral part? Give me the creeps, funerals do," admitted the Pride of the Muldoons.

"We will most probably not be in time for the funeral,"

said Zarkon. "Ace, we will take the *Silver Ghost* again, since we have to bring the location-finder home, and it would be too big for any of the cars. Let's go, gentlemen, Miss Grimshaw!"

"Ohboyoboyoboyoboy, a little action at last, maybe!" burbled Scorchy Muldoon zestfully.

The helicopter flight across the city and out to the late Jerred Streiger's mansion in the exclusive Long Island suburb of Holmwood was brief and uneventful.

Ace Harrigan brought the big chopper down on the same unused tennis court he employed as a makeshift chopper landing pad earlier. They piled out one by one and walked around to the front of the house.

Their timing was almost perfect. Long, black, air-conditioned limousines were pulling up smoothly before the front entrance to disgorge dark-suited mourners returning from the funeral of the murdered millionaire. Among these, Zarkon recognized Constable Oglethorpe Gibbs, remarkably fresh and dapper for once, and his huge, cheerful nephew. They greeted him respectfully and Constable Gibbs drew the Lord of the Unknown aside for a few moments of confidential conversation.

"What was *that* all about?" inquired Doctor Ernestine Grimshaw, as Zarkon rejoined his comrades.

"A call from Ricks," said the Omega Man. "He knew the funeral was this afternoon and called Gibbs on the chance we might be out here. An item of information has come through from Palfrey of Z5 in London, acting in co-operation with Interpol."

"Something important?" demanded the girl interestedly.

"Any morsel of information we can acquire on this case is of some importance," said Zarkon evasively.

"How's that?"

"I have my suspicions, but little evidence," admitted the

Man from Tomorrow. "Every datum I can gather tightens the noose about the suspect's throat another knot."

The girl looked at him blankly.

"Do you mean—you know who the Grim Reaper *is?*" she breathed incredulously.

"Of course," said Zarkon absently. "I have known his identity for two days now. But proving my suspicions, well, that is another matter—"

The girl was about to ask another question, and a more pointed one, but just then a large, jovial, red-faced man in impeccable mourning clothes came bustling up with a pale, sandy-haired, subdued young man in tow.

"Prince Zarkon, how charming to see you again! Pity it has to be under such unhappy circumstances," he said heartily.

"Mr. Seaton," Zarkon acknowledged his greetings. They shook hands, then Seaton gestured at the downcast young man at his side.

"I don't believe you have met Mr. Caleb Streiger, have you? Cal, m'boy, this is His Highness, Prince Zarkon of Novenia. He has been investigating your uncle's demise."

Zarkon exchanged greetings with the gangling young man, who seemed to be all elbows and knees, and introduced both men to Ernestine Grimshaw. The guests who had attended the funeral of Jerred Streiger were by this time trooping into the house, where Sherrinford the butler and one of the maids collected their hats and topcoats. Zarkon, the Omega men, and Dr. Grimshaw were the last to enter the mansion.

As the red-faced lawyer came bustling up, Zarkon excused himself briefly to visit the restroom. When he rejoined the company a few moments later, Josiah Seaton was beaming in his self-important and slightly pompous manner. Casting a pointed glance around the group so as to count heads and make certain everyone was present, Seaton cleared his throat with a loud harrumph, gathering the attention of the mourners, who were a group composed principally of Streiger's household staff.

"I believe we are all here, now, all of us who are mentioned in the will, that is," said Josiah Seaton in his expansive manner. "May I suggest that we go in to the study and I will read the document in question."

One by one they entered the big, book-lined room and settled themselves on the chairs and divans, while the lawyer carried his raincoat and briefcase to a large desk. Setting down the briefcase at his feet, he snapped it open and withdrew an important-looking document therefrom. This he opened with a crackle of thick paper, cleared his throat, and glanced around one last time to make certain he had their full and undivided attention.

Zarkon, who had lingered behind with Constable Gibbs for a few moments, quietly entered and took a chair near the door.

Then Josiah Seaton began to read aloud the last will and testament of Jerred Streiger.

CHAPTER 24

The Grim Reaper Unmasked

After a while, Scorchy Muldoon exchanged an eloquent glance with Nick Naldini, and politely smothered a yawn behind the palm of one hand. If Zarkon had hoped to learn anything of interest or of value, or if he had thought that the will of Jerred Streiger was likely to contain any last-minute surprises, it became increasingly obvious as time wore on that the Lord of the Unknown was going to be disappointed.

The bequests contained in Streiger's will were exactly as Josiah Seaton had predicted they would be—which ought to have come as no surprise to anyone, come to think of it, since it had been Seaton himself who had drawn the will up for Streiger in the first place.

Decent but unsurprising sums of money were settled upon Mrs. Callahan, the housekeeper, Sherrinford, the butler, Borg, Streiger's bodyguard, Pipkin, the gatekeeper, Canning, the deceased millionaire's private secretary, and most of the other servants on the staff of Twelve Oaks, including, of course, Chandra Lal, who had been Streiger's valet. These bequests were generous enough in their way, but comprised only a small fraction of the total value of the estate, the bulk of which, including Jerred Streiger's majority stockholdings in the Worldwide Steel Corporation, went to the Streiger Foundation itself. As for the murdered man's only close living relative, his nephew Caleb, whom as Seaton had in-

formed Prince Zarkon earlier the murdered millionaire had
disliked, he received only a modest annual stipend, together
with the property and furnishings of Twelve Oaks itself. The
shy, awkward young man flushed, bowed his head slightly,
and rubbed his bony-knuckled hands together nervously
when his portion of the estate was read off. But whether this
was an angry reaction to being so largely cut out of the
Streiger wealth, or young Caleb's natural reaction to being
singled out in public, it was hard to say, although privately
Scorchy and the others would have chosen the latter as most
likely.

In his fulsome, hearty manner, the red-faced lawyer read
the document through to its end, cleared his throat again,
asked if there were any questions, received only a politely
negative murmur as reply, and stood up, stuffing the will
back into his briefcase, which he placed up on the desk in
preparation for his departure.

"Well, then, if there are no pertinent questions, I believe
that will be all," he said pleasantly. "I'm sure the members of
the staff will wish to return to their duties, unless Mr. Caleb
Streiger has instructions, ah, to the contrary?"

"No, no, that's p-perfectly all right," said that young man
hurriedly.

"Well, then. Thank you all for your time—ah—Your
Highness has a question?" The lawyer sounded politely in-
quisitive, for just then Zarkon had gotten to his feet and
began walking to the center of the room.

"There is one more thing, Mr. Seaton, if you don't mind,"
said the Man of Mysteries quietly.

"No, of course not, my dear sir! Please go ahead . . ."

"Thank you." Zarkon turned to look at the mourners, who
regarded him blankly. Scorchy and Nick exchanged a
mystified glance, then shrugged in unison and turned to hear
what their chief had to say.

"As some of you probably know, the Knickerbocker City
Homicide Bureau has called me in to assist the local authori-

ties in investigating the death of the late Mr. Streiger," said Zarkon in a low voice. "There is considerable evidence to suggest that the death of Jerred Streiger was not due to natural causes, but was a deliberate act of murder on the part of person or persons unknown. Since all of you gathered here knew the deceased man, and are naturally concerned that his murderer or murderers be brought to justice and are made to pay for their crimes, it seems only fitting and proper that I share with you now the results of my investigation thus far."

The deep, quiet, perfectly modulated tones of the Man of Mysteries, his commanding mien and piercing magnetic gaze, held the crowd of mourners as might some seasoned actor or practiced orator or brilliant trial attorney. He stepped forward to a position toward the front of the room where they could all see and hear him without difficulty.

"My first task," began Zarkon, "was of course to ascertain to my own satisfaction that Jerred Streiger had, in fact, been murdered. While law-enforcement officers do not ordinarily suspect the victim of a heart attack to have died from other than natural causes, there were curious circumstances surrounding Mr. Streiger's death which suggested the presence of a crime. Not the least of these, certainly, was the fact that the dead man had been for some time receiving threatening letters. This is no particular secret, I am sure, to those of you who were Mr. Streiger's employees. The last of these threats, received on the day of his death, predicted the very hour of his demise.

"Now, there are, of course, ways in which a heart attack can be caused by deliberate means, but these are generally used in those murders which are carefully planned to look like natural deaths. I refer to certain drugs or poisons which can precipitate a heart seizure, or to the injection of an air-bubble into the blood-veins, or to the use of a chemical agent which causes a blood clot to form. In the case of Jerred Streiger, circumstances would seem to rule out these methods. His physician found no trace of any foreign substance in the corpse, and the drugs or poisons which could have brought on a heart attack by artificial means all leave a chemical residue in the body. The only exception to this is the use of curare, the poison employed by South American Indian tribes to envenom their blowgun darts; the presence of curare in the body, however, can generally be detected by its effect upon the cells of the brain. And, as for the injection of an air-bubble into the blood-vein, that would of course leave a puncture-wound, which, although no bigger than a pin-prick, could still be detected in the course of an autopsy. So in the case of Jerred Streiger, I had to look still further to discover the method of the murder.

"I know of only one other way of inducing a blood clot to form, which I will describe presently. This particular method of murder is rather intricate and complicated, and requires the use of an instrument within fifteen feet of the victim. When I first examined the murder room I carefully measured off that distance in all directions from the spot on which Jerred Streiger collapsed. The room is so arranged, of such proportions, and the furniture situated in such a manner, that there was only one place where the murderer could have concealed himself from view and yet have been within range to bring his weapon to bear upon his victim: he would have had to stand in the flower beds outside the room, just beyond the French windows. From that position he could have used his device, even though the drapes were drawn. And, such is the position of the table lamp, that it would have thrown Jerred Streiger's shadow on the drapes so that, even although he could not actually see into the room, the murderer would know precisely where to aim his weapon.

"Therefore, I opened the windows and looked outside. There, exactly where I expected to find them, I discovered the imprint of the feet of an unknown person. The size of the footprints was unusually small, suggesting the murderer to have either been a rather small man, or a woman or a child. But the prints were those of a man's shoes, and not a woman's, and there are no children on the property. From this evidence, and from the fact that the impression of the murderer's shoes in the soft loam, which were pressed considerably deeper into the earth at the toe than at the heel, suggesting that the murderer had to stand virtually on his tiptoes in order to see the shadow on the drapes and bring his weapon to bear, all combined to convince me that the murderer was a very short man with very small feet. When I questioned each and every member of the staff in turn I discovered that the gardener's boy, a young Chinese named Pei Ling, matched each of these requirements. I also learned that he was one of the most recent members of the staff here at Twelve Oaks. He seemed the most likely suspect."

"Do you mean," demanded the lawyer incredulously, "that a teen-aged gardener's boy is the Grim Reaper?"

Zarkon shook his head negatively.

"I did not say that, Mr. Seaton. The boy, Pei Ling, was the actual murderer; but the Grim Reaper is another person entirely, and would have to be."

"Pray continue, then. And forgive the interruption."

Zarkon nodded and resumed his narration.

"My organization uses a small radio broadcasting instrument which has been miniaturized to a size no bigger than a pinhead," he said. "Using one of the little tricks of misdirection taught me by my associate, Mr. Naldini, a former stage magician, I attached one of these tiny instruments to the clothing worn by the Chinese boy. Since I could not be absolutely positive that it was he and no other had been the murderer, I attached a similar instrument to the garments of every member of the staff. I then summoned two more of my associates from my headquarters with a new radio location-finder attuned to the carrier-wave broadcast by these instruments, and we kept watch. If any member of the staff should leave suddenly or unexpectedly, which might be an indication of his or her guilt, it was our plan to follow that person's movements by means of the map-grid of this device.

"As some of you know, Pei Ling did in fact leave Twelve Oaks not very long after Mr. Streiger's death. Through the use of my instrument we managed to track him to the outskirts of the Chinatown section of the City, but unfortunately he passed beyond the limited range of my set and so we were unable to follow his movements beyond that point. But it seemed very likely that my suspicions regarding Pei Ling's culpability in the murder were now confirmed. An additional confirmation came when I learned the fact that another man of wealth and important holdings, similarly threatened by notes of the same tenor, who died of similar causes under similar circumstances, had also just before the advent of these threatening letters added a person of Oriental extraction to his staff. That person, I later learned, had been acquired through the identical employment service through which Jerred Streiger had hired the boy Pei Ling. It would seem that we were confronted with a Chinese gang of criminals, such as had once plagued the city police during the era of the Tong wars."

"I gather from your words, then," said Josiah Seaton interestedly, "that this Grim Reaper, the mastermind behind these murders, is an Oriental gangland leader?"

"Not necessarily," murmured Zarkon. "Although such could indeed have been the case. But there was a certain criminal organization, formerly active in Knickerbocker City's Chinatown district, whose leader had been a sage or savant of venerable authority among the citizens of the district: a mysterious figure held in superstitious awe by the residents. He himself was long-since dead, but there was no reason why his place could not have been taken by another. Since this individual dwelt in seclusion in a secret place, there was no real argument against his successor being of Caucasian descent, since even his followers saw him but rarely.

"The decisive bit of evidence came into our hands from the very brave deed of Mr. Streiger's personal valet, Chandra Lal, who happened to see Pei Ling fleeing from the estate, decided his actions were of a suspicious nature, and took it upon himself to follow the boy to his hideout, this secret headquarters of which I have been speaking. Chandra Lal managed to inform us by telephone of the address before he was taken prisoner by the gang. Unfortunately, the building is in a part of Chinatown where the houses are connected by a veritable maze of tunnels and secret passages; so most of the gang managed to escape during the early hours of this morning when the police staged their raid. Among those who got away was the Grim Reaper himself. Fortunately for the cause of justice, however, his escape was futile, for by this time conclusive evidence has come to light which establishes his true identity beyond question."

The rosy-faced lawyer blinked in surprise.

"Do you mean—you know who this murderous fiend actually is?" he gasped.

Zarkon nodded, his face grimly expressionless. The mourners exchanged sidelong glances in which excitement and apprehension were curiously mingled. It was almost as if each of them suspected that the person seated next to him might in secret be the sinister criminal mastermind who struck from nowhere with the unseen power of the Invisible Death.

"Well, then, good heavens, man—tell us! *Who?*" demanded lawyer Josiah Seaton.

"There sits the Grim Reaper," said Zarkon, leveling a hand.

Consternation showed in the pale, tense, excited features of those present as they craned their heads around in order to ascertain who it was among them whom Prince Zarkon had accused.

And then gasps of amazement burst from the astounded throng as they realized the identity of the individual singled out by Zarkon's pointing hand.

That person flushed and stammered, fidgeting with hands and feet, crimsoning as he became the object of their concentrated gaze.

It was the murdered man's nephew, Caleb Streiger!

Constable Oglethorpe Gibbs, who happened to be seated directly behind the nervous and rabbity young man, sprang to his feet and seized him by the arm in his strong, calloused hands. In a moment a metallic *click* sounded through the hubbub and uproar of excited voices, as the law officer locked the awkward youth's bony wrists in a pair of strong handcuffs.

"Well, now I git it!" snorted that remarkably homely and slovenly officer. "Thet-thar is why Mister Prince Zarkon asked me t'pick a chere right behind this 'un. Young feller, yer unner arrest fer th' murder o' Jerred Streiger, late o' this county. Enythang yew say is likely t'be used aginst yew, yew murderin' young skunk, yew! Redneck, fetch me moh car."

"Faster'n a houn'dawg kin skritch his ear, Oggie," said the strapping young deputy with a cheerful grin. Then, noting the fierce expression on the other's knobby visage, he amended his words hastily. "*Uncle* Oggie, thet is!"

Through the stir and chatter, one figure sat motionless as if completely paralyzed with amazement. It was the corpulent, red-faced, smooth-tongued attorney, Josiah Seaton. Rarely was the clever lawyer at a loss for words: but this was one of those times. The expression of surprise on his normally jolly and well-fleshed features was so acute as to suggest slack-jawed idiocy.

"Young Cal Streiger," he gurgled, eyes goggling blankly. "Well, I never. Why . . . who'd have thought the young idiot had enough brains to be a master-criminal! Never in a million years . . ."

CHAPTER 25

The Last Nail in the Coffin

Eventually, the dazed lawyer recovered from his surprise and regained something of his composure.

"Quiet, please! Everybody please calm down," he boomed, his expansive voice cutting through the noise. As the mourners quieted, Josiah Seaton wiped his streaming brow with a silk handkerchief and turned to Prince Zarkon.

"Well, sir, I imagine there's no question but that Your Highness has sufficient evidence to back up these astounding accusations, although for the very life of me I can't imagine what proof there could be of such an incredible thing. I've known this boy all his life, and, quite frankly, well . . ."

The portly lawyer let his words trail away uncomfortably. Prince Zarkon smiled.

"Yes, I believe I have all the evidence I need to convict the criminal," he said. "Every piece of evidence we gather in the course of investigating a crime is like another nail in the criminal's coffin. Oddly enough, it was you yourself, Mr. Seaton, who inadvertently managed to supply me with one of the most important clues in the case, although I hardly recognized it as such at the time."

"I did? What was that?"

"His address. When we first discussed the case in your office a day or two ago, perhaps you will remember. You told me that Streiger's nephew was a rather unworldly young man, whose one and only vice was a consuming passion for radio, in which field he was something of an inventor."

"Oh yes, of course; I remember the occasion well. But what does that have to do with . . . ?"

"With the murder? The only method of causing a blood clot without leaving a chemical residue in the bloodstream or causing a mark on the body is a little-known side-effect of radio short waves. From extremely close range, short waves in the so-called 'hard' radio frequencies can cause the blood to clot. But it would take a radio experimenter of considerable expertise to know how to do it, and to devise an instrument able to cause this effect. Cal Streiger, who holds several small patents on short wave radio modifications, is just the sort of inventor who could concoct such a device. And that is the secret of the Invisible Death, a portable broadcasting unit in the hard frequencies."

"But are you *certain* that was the method used?" pressed Josiah Seaton dubiously.

"Quite certain, because while such short waves leave no mark of any kind on the human body, they react chemically with ordinary panes of glass, such as that used in French windows. They cause a minor discoloration similar to that caused by prolonged exposure to desert sunshine. If you have ever seen a piece of glass in the desert, which has lain out in the open for several years, you will know the peculiar iridescence such prolonged exposure to strong sunlight causes in glass, even bottle-glass. That iridescent coloring was first noticed by Charles Tiffany, the famous *art nouveau* craftsman, who strove to produce a similar opalescence in his stained glass vases and lampshades. He did it during the *art nouveau* era by chemical means; today, modern art glass in that style is rendered iridescent by brief periods of exposure to radio short waves."

"Incredible. Simply incredible!"

"And if any further evidence is needed, my friend Detective Inspector Ricks should be gathering it right now. I talked to him about noontime and we planned a police raid on young Streiger's workshop. We should find prototype models of the Invisible Death projector, plans or blueprints or schematics, or at least notes on the progress of his experiments in perfecting the weapon."

Josiah Seaton was beyond words at this point. He merely nodded helplessly.

"And, of course, you gave me a second clue during our brief chat in your office," added Zarkon. "You mentioned that his workshop was on Graumann Street. And Graumann Street is on the other side of the block from the street on which Wang Foo's Tea Shop stands. This tea shop is the main entrance to the secret hideout of the Grim Reaper; I have no doubt that when Ricks' men start breaking through the walls they will find that at least one of the secret tunnels leading from the hideout comes out in the back room of Caleb Streiger's workshop on Graumann Street, probably concealed by a sliding panel or something of that nature. Ricks checked the street address for me: the workshop is less than forty-five yards from Wang Foo's Tea Shop. They are actually in the same building, for the two buildings were built back to back, each facing out on a different street."

Redneck Pickett thrust his head in the door and signaled to Oglethorpe Gibbs.

"Car's aroun' front, Unk," he said.

"On yer feet, yew," growled Constable Oglethorpe Gibbs. The unhappy young man climbed to his feet and stumbled out of the room, accompanied by the Constable. He still looked unprepossessing: a gangling and shy and awkward young man, who hardly fitted anyone's mental picture of that mysterious crime mastermind, the Grim Reaper.

Looking after him, Josiah Seaton sighed dispiritedly, picking up his briefcase and draping his topcoat over his arm.

"I still can't believe it," he wheezed. "Cal Streiger! A super-criminal . . . I'd never have guessed the dear boy had it in him. The gumption, I mean, and, well, the *cleverness*."

"Well, he didn't do it all alone, of course," Zarkon said quietly. "You helped more than a little."

The room froze in utter silence at this quietly-voiced verbal bombshell.

The color drained from Seaton's face, leaving it pale and unhealthy-looking and blotched. The lawyer said nothing, merely watched Prince Zarkon with bright, wary eyes. They were sharp and fearful, those eyes. They were the eyes of a small animal caught in a trap.

"Save for the act of a homicidal maniac," Zarkon said, "the crime of murder is never completely divorced from the profit motive. Even a crime of passion involves personal gain; if a wife murders a husband, or a husband a wife, the motive may generally be found in the matter of inheritance, or insurance money, or merely the wish to clear the ground for a more desirable marriage. It was much the same in this case. While Caleb Streiger stood to inherit the house and grounds—whose value would amount to a comfortable fortune—the only other real beneficiary from the death of Jerred Streiger is the Streiger Foundation, of which you are the Director-in-Chief.

"This was actually the most vital clue into the entire mystery, and it was one of the very first things I learned, long before it meant anything to me," said Zarkon slowly. "Think back to our brief meeting in your office. A chance gesture knocked a large malachite ashtray off your desk. I picked it up and replaced it, and at the time I noticed without really paying any attention to the inscription carved in the base. It was presented to you by the Board of Directors of the Foundation upon your election to that office. Now, according to an informant on the Stock Exchange, the Board only meets three times a year to rubber-stamp decisions made by the Director-in-Chief. Yourself. You run the Foundation, control its monies, plan its investments. It was you who would most benefit from the death of Jerred Streiger, not his nephew.

"This morning, when I talked with Ricks on the phone, I got the news I had been waiting for. Interpol finally pierced through the web of interlocking directorships and dummy corporations, to the real owner of the Pan-Global Corporation—the Swiss conglomerate to which the Grim Reaper demanded his future victims sign over their holdings. It is a subsidiary of the Streiger Foundation, solely under your control. And officials of the state licensing bureau informed me that the Foundation similarly holds the controlling interest in another company, the Herrolds Employment Bureau, which is the firm from which Pei Ling and the two other Chinese murderers were hired by Pulitzer Haines, Jerred Streiger, and Ogilvie Mather. Every trail I followed in this case leads back to you, Mr. Seaton. You are the power behind the throne—the *real* mastermind. You are the Grim Reaper."

"I underestimated you, Prince Zarkon," whispered Josiah Seaton through stiff, colorless lips.

"You did not find it difficult to persuade Caleb Streiger to help you kill his uncle. You've known that unfortunate young man all his life, and you were the friendly parental-substitute to which he turned when his uncle rebuffed him and cut him off. You have a glib tongue and a winning manner. It must have been child's play for you to gradually talk the boy into murder. As for Pulitzer Haines, he was a decoy, I suspect. You had him killed because you had no connection with him whatsoever. He was hard as nails, or had that reputation among the stockbrokers; he would never yield to threats. He died, so that when Streiger died, it would seem as if a cunning criminal was attempting to wrest a fortune from an entire group of wealthy and influential men—"

"That's where you're wrong," said Josiah Seaton. And now for the first time a certain warmth and vigor crept into his hollow tones. "Pulitzer Haines, Jerred Streiger, and Ogilvie Mather were the principal members in a secret group of powerful investors who caused a fluctuation in the Market which ruined me, wiped me out, left me penniless. They did not intend to destroy me, of course; they never realized that my holdings were among those destroyed when they caused the

Market to wobble ever so slightly. They made a fortune from that wobble; I lost everything I had—everything except my brain, my will, my cunning. I hated them, and would have destroyed them one by one. In so doing, I gained possession of Streiger's vast holdings. I would have gained control over Mather's holdings, too, because he was weak. He would have given in. So would the next two on my list, also members of the group. I was too old to start over, Zarkon. I determined to become wealthier than ever before, and to destroy my destroyers in the process. And I would have succeeded, had it not been for you. I underestimated you. *But no more than you have underestimated me—*"

With those words, Seaton let fall the topcoat which he had draped over his arm—the arm holding the briefcase. Masked by the coat, no eye had seen his hand dip into the open briefcase and draw therefrom the strange tubular glittering radio projector which he now held clenched in one hand like the deadly weapon it was. Swiveling the instrument about, he said harshly: "Let no one move! From this range I can cause a clot in anyone in the room—and they'll be dead of a heart attack within seconds."

Scorchy swore a fierce Gaelic oath, hands curling into hard fists. But Nick Naldini laid his hand on the little boxer's arm, restraining him.

"Easy, boy! The chief's right up front. He'll get it first if anybody tries anything."

"You're right, my Mephistophelean friend," snarled Seaton, showing his teeth in a tigerish grin. The strange radio-gun in his fat fist was pointed unswervingly at Prince Zarkon's heart. "If any of you so much as move, it is Prince Zarkon who will be the first to die the Invisible Death!"

Zarkon faced him unflinchingly, his black magnetic eyes quiet and somber.

"You are wrong again, Seaton. I did not in the least underestimate you. I came to this showdown fully prepared."

"Eh?"

"You are no expert in the radio field, unlike your hapless dupe, Caleb Streiger. So you are probably unaware that an alloy of cadmium and beryllium is proof to radio in the short wave lengths. My associate, Menlo Parker, constructed for me an undergarment of overlapping thin plates of this alloy, which I put on under my clothing just before entering this room. Perhaps you will recall that, before entering, I went to the restroom? At that time I donned this protective garment. Wearing it, your radio projector cannot harm me in the slightest."

Seaton blinked, fierce wary eyes suddenly going dull.

"Eh?" he repeated, his face sagging. His rotund figure had been tense with coiled energy, like a predatory thing. Now it seemed heavy and unresponsive, and his movements were listless.

"You cannot hurt me," Zarkon repeated in a level voice. "And I am standing close enough to you that before you can turn it on another person, I can be on you. I am younger and stronger than you are; you are no match for me in a struggle. Put the instrument down and surrender yourself. Do it now!"

The probing eyes of black magnetic fire held the dull gaze of the heavy-faced lawyer. All animation seemed to have gone out of Seaton. For a moment, he said nothing. Then he sighed heavily, and his hand wavered and fell. The radio weapon slipped from his loose grip and crashed to the floor, delicate ray tubes shattering. And people all over the room started to breathe again.

"Thank God," said Ricks hoarsely from the doorway leading into the hall. The detective stepped into view, holstering the revolver he held gripped in one hand. "I had a bead on him from the door, but you were between us, Prince Zarkon, and I was afraid to shoot." He took out a pair of cuffs and snapped them on the wrists of the lawyer, who stood unresisting, staring dully into nothingness with empty eyes. "Damn clever trick, that cadmium underwear," said the detective feelingly.

Zarkon permitted himself a rare smile.

"I fear I am guilty of a slight prevarication," he chuckled.

"How's that? I thought—"

"There is no metal known which reflects short waves in the manner I mentioned."

Ricks swore and turned pale and bit his lips. "You mean that was just—a bluff?"

"I'm afraid so," said Zarkon. And it was all over.

After the police had taken Josiah Seaton and Caleb Streiger away to the lockup in town, the Omega men dismantled the location-finder and packed it away in the *Silver Ghost*. It was time to go.

Nick Naldini and Scorchy Muldoon tried heroically to get a date with Doctor Ernestine Grimshaw, or at least to secure her telephone number. But the pretty blond physician fended off their advances in a casual, absent-minded way, almost by unconscious instinct.

At first the two didn't catch on. Then they saw that old, familiar look in the girl's big blue eyes whenever she glanced at Prince Zarkon, which she did as frequently as she could. The lanky magician and the feisty little prize-fighter exchanged a mutinous look between them, but sighed resignedly. It had happened many times before; doubtless, it would happen many times in the future.

"Sure, an' once a good-lookin' colleen sets her eyes on th' chief, it's good-by to the loikes of yez and me, me bucko," said the Pride of the Muldoons woefully, lapsing into his brogue again. The Irish lingo always caused a distinct pain to the long-legged magician. He groaned and clutched his brow with a theatrical gesture.

"Look out, lads," he groaned in hollow, sepulchral tones, "here comes that road company Barry Fitzgerald act again!" Scorchy sniffed, bristling; scarcely conscious of the accent into which he fell in moments of stress, it always "got his Irish up" when Nick Naldini made a crack of that nature.

"Lissen here, you third-rate imitation of John Carradine playing Count Dracula," he growled in pointed allusion to his chum's Mephisto-like resemblance to that actor in full Transylvanian make-up and rig, "you—you hack stand-in for Houdini, you—"

Stung by the slighting reference to the famous escape artist, whose memory he solemnly venerated, Nick gave vent to a roar of fury and began a new series of spluttering insults on the theme of Scorchy's noticeable lack of inches. Arguing vehemently, the two sauntered off toward the men loading the helicopter.

Ace Harrigan and Doc Jenkins watched them go, grinning fondly.

"Those two take the cake," chuckled the big, dumb-looking man with the outsized feet and miracle brain. "They always get to fighting over a cutie, and when she gives 'em the cold shoulder and starts makin' sheep's-eyes at the chief, they get into a squabble and enjoy themselves so much they forget all about the cutie! I always feel sorry for the girl, though . . . the chief never gives 'em a tumble, so they come out empty-handed."

"Not this time," grinned Ace Harrigan. The handsome young aviator looked as smug as the cat who had just stolen the key to the canary cage. His brown eyes were sparkling with repressed glee. Doc gave him a baffled glance and made an interrogative motion with his huge, pale, freckled hands.

"I got a date with the blond sawbones myself," chuckled the crack test pilot. "She's a sucker for prime ribs and a good dry martini, and it just happens I know the best steak joint in town. They got a guy behind the bar to whom the mixing of a dry martini is an art form, too. So don't worry about the gal M.D., she's in for a snazzy night on the town with yours truly—"

Just then Menlo Parker came ambling up. The skinny little scientist looked miffed.

"What are you two bums up to, loitering around here,

leaving all the loadin'-up to the rest of us?" he demanded suspiciously.

"Ace was just tellin' me he's got a date lined up with—" Doc Jenkins started to explain, but Menlo cut him off with a curt word before the big man could finish.

"Well, that's tough; cancel it, Ace. The chief just got a call relayed through from Blanco Grande—he wants to fly down there tonight. Somethin' big is brewin'—"

"For the luvva—from where?" demanded Ace Harrigan sharply.

"Blanco Grande. Capital of one of them vest-pocket banana republics south of the border; Hidalgo, that's the name of the joint. Seems they got some spooky stuff goin' on . . ."

His voice trailed off into silence as an expression of excruciating suffering convulsed the handsome features of the aviator. Ace clapped one hand to his brow with a muffled groan and went tottering off in the direction of the pert blond doctor to make his lame apologies. Doc Jenkins wheezed, scarlet with mirth. Menlo turned a sharp, suspicious eye on his huge hulking friend.

"What's the matter with you?" he demanded. "Jeez, you and Ace! Both actin' like a couple of loonies, I swear! What's up with you guys, anyway?"

"Nothing," choked Doc Jenkins, wiping tears of laughter from his pale blue eyes. "It's just that Ace was chortling, just now, about gettin' one up on Nick and Scorchy, and here you come along with the bad news. And those two guys got the last laugh, after all!"

He wandered off toward the big cargo chopper, wheezing with mirth. Menlo watched him go with an expression of disapproving bafflement on his wrinkled, prune-like features. Finally, the little physicist shrugged bony shoulders and gave up trying to figure it out.

"Buncha loonies around here," he said to himself with a

sniff, and went over to the helicopter, which was soon to depart for a new adventure in a far-off land.

Wherever decent, law-abiding, honest men and women were plagued by uncanny menace or weird, inexplicable crimes, there the Omega men were ready and eager to venture, even if it meant a flight to the farthest corners of the world. Were it not for their willingness to fare bravely into the face of death, and do battle against mysterious forces, the world would not for very long enjoy its relative freedom from such fears.

But they were willing, and would always be. And soon the *Silver Ghost* soared into the late afternoon sky, bearing the Lord of the Unknown and his lieutenants to the beginning of a new and even more exciting adventure.

THE END

But Zarkon, Lord of the Unknown,
and the Omega men will return in

"THE VOLCANO OGRE"